FAKING IT

Also by Angel M. Hunter

Sister Girls
Around the Way Girls

FAKING IT

ANGEL M. HUNTER

URBAN BOOKS LLC
www.urbanbooks.net

Urban Books
74 Andrews Avenue
Wheatley Heights, NY 11798

ISBN 1-893196-47-X

First Printing June 2006
Printed in the United States of America

10 9 8 7 6 5 4 3 2 1

Submit Wholesale Orders to:
Kensington Publishing Corp.
C/O Penguin Group (USA) Inc.
Attention: Order Processing
405 Murray Hill Parkway
East Rutherford, NJ 07073-2316
Phone: 1-800-526-0275
Fax: 1-800-227-9604

Acknowledgments

I give thanks to the Almighty and His Son. The past two years You have pulled me through so many changes and challenges, and for this I give thanks. I have the faith of a mustard seed, and I know You will continue to carry me over and through.

My love goes out to Tony Irby, my husband, lover and best friend; also to my son, my little man, Anthony Irby.

Roy Glenn and Carl Weber, I thank you for doing what you do and letting me be a part of it.

This book is dedicated to my readers. I thank you for taking my words and making them powerful. You are appreciated. Please grab hold of the messages I try to slip in.

I also dedicate this to those who are tired, those who are fed up with grinning and pretending, tired of faking the funk. It's time to be real, to be honest with yourself about who you are and what you want to do. Don't go by someone else's script. Write your own part and be true to self. When you do this, you'll be amazed by what follows.

Oh, and always make time for yourself, even if it's just 15 minutes a day. Don't take on more than you can handle. Your time is your time and you must be the one to decide what you will use your energy on.

Write me at msangelhunter@aol.com. Can't wait to hear from you.

Peace and Blessings,
Angel M. Hunter-Irby

LAYLA SIMONE

"How does it feel?" he asked as he played with my nipples, caressing them with the tips of his fingers. Then he ran his tongue across one and down my stomach. He was getting ready to do what I loved most—eat the coochie.

"Good," I told him, feeling guilty. Here my man was making love to me, and my mind was wandering. Now you know that wasn't right, but I couldn't help it.

I'd been so preoccupied lately. Normally when the oral began, my body took over. Nothing could disturb the pleasure I knew was about to take place, but the last couple of times we made love, it was almost like I wasn't there. I think I was going through a depression, having a breakdown, or going through an early mid-life crisis. Why? Because I wasn't living my life the way I wanted to.

I was so tired of living in this small-ass town with no hope, no future. Not saying I wasn't talented or couldn't be whatever I chose, it was just that in Branch Park, New Jersey, a small town with a graduating class of 200 where everyone knew everyone and everyone had everyone's man and woman, I didn't see it happening. I was born and raised in this common town—that's what this town was, a common town with common people—meaning, there was one hospital, one high school, and one major department store. For excitement you had to go one state over.

Me? I'd always felt different. I was more diverse in talents, ideas, and goals than others and often felt like I didn't quite belong. I'd always wanted more than most people. My friends and family called me a dreamer, but you know what, dreams can come true.

Look at Oprah Winfrey, Whitney Houston, and Terri McMillan, just to name a few. I'm sure before they had the success they enjoy now, it was a dream. Something they thought and fantasized about. Now they're millionaires—people know their names, watch their shows, listen to their music, and read their books—so I knew my dreams weren't futile, like those non-believers would've had me think if I was weak in the mind. I shouldn't say non-believers—that's too strong a word; maybe I should say those individuals who were contented, comfortable, and settled. But, you see, I wasn't; I knew what I wanted and was tired of putting it on hold. It was time to do something about it.

You may wonder, why did I put it on hold? Well, I have to be honest with you and tell you it was no one's fault but my own. I wanted to please everyone, from my father to my mother, from my brothers to my boyfriend. Seeking approval was what I did best.

Before I go on, I'll give you an example of me trying to fit in and be liked. It happened in junior high school. You know how there's the cool crowd and the whack crowd? Well, me, I was stuck in the middle, and that definitely wasn't where I wanted to be. One day I overheard the girls I wanted so much to be like talking about how they got drunk the night before. I decided to show them how down I was, being inexperienced and all in the life of alcohol. That night I went home and went through the liquor cabinet. I decided to take a bottle of wine and gin to school. Mind you, I had no idea what kind of effect it would have on me. All I could think about was the attention I would receive and how it would be about *me* for the first time.

The next day finally came, and as I was walking to the bus stop, my brother, Ali, realized I was switching my bag from shoulder to shoulder. "Let me carry your bag," he said.

"Nah, I got it." There was no way I was letting him carry it; I didn't want to get busted before I even got to school.

"It seems a little heavy."

"I said I got it—dag!"

"Damn, I was just trying to be nice."

"Well, you don't have to be nice all the time."

You see, Ali was a gentleman, and the girls loved him for it. He was always carrying someone's books, helping them out with their homework and opening doors.

"And you don't have to be so rude."

I apologized, but still chose to carry my book bag.

When school started I tried to figure out the best time to tell my friends about my little surprise. I chose lunchtime because the teachers wouldn't be around. I had to be slick about it. I knew that around this time the girls went behind the school to smoke cigarettes, so I decided to go out as well. Out I went and glanced around, spotting them almost immediately. They were all dressed in hip-huggers, white T-shirts, and sneakers, looking like the clique they were. I made sure I sat close to them before opening my book bag, taking out a soda, and, on the not-so-sneaky tip, pouring some gin into the can.

"Whatcha got there?" one of the girls asked.

"Some gin and a little wine," I told her in a nonchalant manner, like it was something I did every day.

Next thing you know, they all gathered around, asking for some. Of course, I gave it to them, thinking this was it—I was now going to be a part of the in-crowd.

Let me tell you, a sister was messed up. At first I wasn't feeling anything. Then out of nowhere the liquor just hit me.

Actually, I think it hit all of us. We were acting so loud and ignorant one of the teachers came over and wanted to know what was going on. No one answered. We all just stood there looking stupid.

One of the younger teachers, Mr. Bell, knew something was up. He took a bottle from one of the girls and sniffed it. "Who brought the liquor to school?"

I thought everyone would remain silent. Do you know those little wenches turned me in? Not only did I get suspended, but when I arrived home I got an ass whipping as well.

Ali picked on me and said, "So that's why you wouldn't let me carry your bag. Stupidity makes a hard ass."

You would think I'd learned my lesson after that, but I didn't. I continued to be a people-pleaser. Eventually I figured out it wasn't the way to live life, that instead of being a follower I needed to be a leader. Okay, I admit, it may have taken until I was an adult and getting hurt to realize it.

What did I see in my future? Well, I saw pure boredom, a simple life, habits, the same routine day in and day out, and achieving what was considered small-town success. I wanted more, I needed more, and I deserved more. I was destined for more.

I believed it when I heard, "We all have a purpose." Mine? I knew that I was to be of service to others and that I should be reaching and teaching people through my writing. I needed to be making money doing something I loved. Words touched me deeply, reaching places in me I never knew existed. I'd been an avid reader ever since I can remember. I can recall as a child being told, "It's time to go to bed," and sneaking and reading under my blanket with a flashlight. I read any and everything I got my hands on—fiction, non-fiction, science fiction, you name it. Reading made me feel smart, like I knew a little more than the average person. If I heard about something or saw something I wanted to learn more about, I headed to the bookstore or the library and read up on it. Of course, from all that reading I eventually started writing.

I wrote just about everything—short stories, poems, and songs. Mind you, they probably weren't that great when I first started, but they definitely got better as I grew older. I went through stages where I wrote about death and suicide. I remember one poem went something like this:

I want to take my life
Where's the knife
Life is no fun
Where's the gun

I was in the sixth grade and when my creative writing teacher read it, he called my mother in for a conference. I tried to explain that it didn't mean anything, it was just a poem, but he wasn't hearing it.

"I'm not taking any chances," he told my mother. "I think you should get her counseling."

"Ma, that's not necessary," I told her. "It's only a poem— I'm not thinking about killing myself."

She looked at me, then back at the counselor. This was the only time I'd ever seen my mother look unsure. She was usually on point, knowing her next move at all times. Taking my face in her hands, she looked me in the eyes and said, "I don't know, baby. Why would you write such things, if it's not how you feel?"

"I think she should see someone as a precaution. If it turns out to be nothing, then I'll be the first to admit my mistake."

So, to a head doctor I went, only to have my mother be told what I knew all along—I was a talented young lady. Oh and yes, the counselor did apologize.

Who am I? What's my name? I forgot to mention it. I just started telling you all my business, and you don't even know me. What's that song by Destiny's Child?—"Say My Name." It was Layla Simone Hudson. I was 5-5, shapely, and full of passion, life, and energy. Honey-complexioned with flawless skin, which I achieved by drinking lots of water, I worked out often and had just received my certification as a personal trainer and aerobics instructor. The way I figured it, I could stay in shape and get paid for it. Plus, I needed to work on the hips and the ass—that's where all the weight dropped. I had to work a little harder to keep the body tight.

Okay I admit it, I was a bit obsessed about my weight, but so were a lot of other women. Let me see . . . what else can I tell you about me? Well, I was an assistant manager in a bookstore. I went to college and studied English, and I substituted occasionally. Simply put, I did a little bit of everything. That's because if I didn't I would have probably lost my mind. I wasn't one to idle or sit around and meditate. I needed to be on the move, making things happen. I read once that there are three types of minds: small, the "I want to's"; medium, the "I'm going to's," and; large, the "I did's." That went to me, the large-minded person.

Friends—did I have any? I'd say no, not really; I had associates. My only true friends were my mother, my two brothers, Keke, Kavan, and my man. Don't get me wrong, I had girls I hung out with from time to time, but those times were few and far between. Why? Well, they wanted to do the same shit over and over, go to the same places, and see the same faces. I was tired of that; I was ready to leave this place and explore the world, see what was out there for me.

You're probably wondering, *Well, damn! Did they finish making love yet? Did she have an orgasm?*—Yes and yes.

Now I had to talk to my man and let him know what was on my mind. I was sure he knew something was up. What was it? Well, I'd decided to move to the West Coast and pursue this writing thing. I'd written four screenplays in the last five years, and with a few changes here and there, I was positive someone was going to be interested in them. I hadn't mentioned this idea to anyone yet, because I was sure it was going to be shot down. I was changing, you see, and people are afraid of change. They want you to stay in the box they put you in and become afraid when you venture out on your own. Some would say I was trying to find myself. I thought I was coming into my own. I refused to let others continue to dictate how I lived my life. It was mine and it was time to take a step forward in the direction I'd wanted to go in for as long as I could remember.

I sincerely hoped that once I told Jaye my plan, he'd decide to come along with me. If he didn't, I still had to do what I had to do, even if that meant leaving him behind.

Saying goodbye is never easy
But moving on
We all must do
Going on with our lives
Not just talking about it
But seeing it through
Move on
My people
Move on

HOW WE GOT STARTED

Jaye and I had been together since we were teenagers—off and on, that is. We met in junior high school. He was the finest brother there. I'm not just saying that either; you can ask anyone. All the girls were after him. He was handsome and smart. I, like all the others, wanted him to be my boyfriend. That was going to be hard to do, or so I thought, when you consider I wasn't having sex and the other girls were. My plan?—to befriend him. Be his friend first, find out his likes and dislikes, and work my magic from there.

It was in biology class that I got my chance. I was failing for the first time, and my teacher requested that I stay after for extra help. I couldn't because I had a part-time job at the mall. The only other option, besides summer school, was to get a tutor. Jaye and I were in the same class, and I knew he was acing it. He always answered the questions right and appeared to be the teacher's favorite. One day after class, I approached him and asked him to be my tutor. To my surprise he said yes. We agreed that he would tutor me twice a week for $15.00. I figured a month would be enough time to make him my man. Yep, I was that confident.

The first evening we met for tutoring I made sure I was

looking sexy. Not too much to make it obvious, but enough to get his attention and still be comfortable. I put on the tightest jeans I could find—I had to lay on the bed to zip them up—and a white T-shirt that hugged the little breast I did have. I then threw on a pair of sandals after I polished my toenails hooker-red. We decided to meet at the library; I wasn't letting him come to my house, not with my brothers there. They knew me so well, they would've been able to tell that I liked him, and I didn't feel like dealing with being teased.

We arrived at the library the same time. My heart was racing.

"What's up?" he said, holding the door open for me.

I looked him up and down. He had changed clothes also. *Was he trying to impress me as well?* "Nothing," I replied. "I just need to pass this class; I don't want to go to summer school."

"Yeah, summer school is not the place to be. Come on, follow me." He moved towards the back of the library.

"I'd follow you to the ends of the earth," I said to myself. I walked behind him and watched his sexy-ass walk, or should I say strut—he walked like a black John Travolta in *Staying Alive.*

Once we sat down he asked me, "What area are you having the most problems in?"

"All of them—I just don't get this biology shit."

We went over some of our past work, and I have to tell you, he almost made it sound interesting. When we were wrapping up, who walks in the library?—Kristina, one of the few white girls who attended our school, and she was headed for our table.

"I wonder if she's coming over here," I thought out loud.

Jaye looked up to see who I was talking about. He smiled when he saw her.

Please don't tell me—

Before I could finish my thought, he stood up and hugged her.

So that's why he changed his clothes.

I stood up and grabbed my books. "I guess I'll leave now," I said with attitude.

"Are you okay?"

"Yeah." I walked away, not even speaking to Kristina. *Damn, her name was even white.* I was furious—one of the finest and smartest boys in my grade was dating a white girl. I wasn't prejudiced; I just believed black should be with black, and white with white. I understood that you couldn't help who you fell in love with. Yes, we all breathed the same air and drank the same water, but something about it just didn't sit right with me. I couldn't get out of there fast enough.

That night I went to bed pissed. "Please God, don't let this be happening," I prayed. I didn't want to believe he was going out like that—dating a white girl. I'd often heard older women talk about the brothers being "snatched by the other side." Well, now I was a witness to it and didn't like it one bit.

The next day in school, I avoided Jaye like the plague, making sure not to go near his locker. By the time sixth period rolled around, which was biology, I was tired of acting bitchy, but wasn't going to back down. When I saw him I rolled my eyes.

He sat next to me. "What's that all about?"

I wanted to go off on his fine ass, but instead I turned my back.

"Damn! Why you being so rude? Rude today, rude yesterday."

"What are you talking about?"

"How you walked off—no 'Thank you,' no 'I appreciate your help,' no 'Hello' to Kristina. Nothing."

"I apologize for not saying thank you, but Kristina is *your* friend, not mine." I knew I was being an ass, but I couldn't help it; this thing called jealously came over me.

"Actually, she's my cousin."

"She's your cousin?—Yeah, right."

"For real . . . by marriage; my uncle is her stepfather."

I just looked at him because if he was lying, it was a good-ass lie.

"You know what—I don't have to explain this to you; I don't even know why you care—you're paying me to tutor you, and that's all." He stood up.

"Wait." I placed my hands on his arm.

He turned around.

"I'm sorry. I'm just bugging—that's all."

"Oh . . . for a second there, I thought you were jealous."

"You wish."

He just laughed . . . like he knew something I didn't.

After our third tutoring session, we started to talk more about ourselves. I guess you could say we became friends. We even started having lunch together. Boy was I disappointed. My goal was to make him my man. It was looking like it would never happen, because Jaye was treating me like a damn sister or best friend. He'd tell me about his dates and the girls he liked. I'm glad he stopped when the discussion came to who he was sexing.

"I don't kiss and tell," was his reply when I questioned him about his sex life.

Hell, I could definitely respect that, because most boys told it all. Even embellished a little . . . especially in high school. I'd just about given up, but he surprised me when Jonathan, a senior, asked me out on a date to a house party. Of course I said yes.

When I told Jaye, he flipped. "Why are you going out with that knucklehead?"

"Why not?" I asked him. He was acting all funny, like he was mad or something. Hell, I thought he'd take it all in stride; after all, we were only *friends*.

"He has a reputation."

"Well, *I* don't."

"Yeah, and we want to keep it that way."

"We?" I rolled my eyes at him. "You trippin'."

"Don't roll your eyes at me. Just be careful—I hear he's an octopus."

"I'll be careful."

Well, you know what—some kind of way, Jaye found out where we were going and showed up. That's right—he crashed the party, and no one seemed to notice but me. I spotted him the second he walked in and decided immediately to milk this moment for what it was worth.

I leaned over and brushed my lips against Jonathan's. He looked at me in surprise and moved closer, placing his lips on mine and putting his tongue in my mouth. I wasn't paying any attention to the kiss, I was too busy looking out the corner of my eye; looking to see if Jaye saw.

I guess he did, because he was heading our way, wearing a frown.

I took a step back from Jonathan and asked him to get us something to drink. By the time he walked away, Jaye was in my face.

"What the hell are you doing?" Jaye asked.

"Wha' you mean, wha' am I doin'?" Of course, my words were slurred—I'd already had two cups of spiked punch. "Havin' a good time."

"I'm taking you home." He grabbed my arm.

I snatched my arm away. "I'm not ready to go home."

He looked me up and down. "How about I call your brothers and tell them you're here drinking and kissing some guy up?"

All hell would certainly break loose if he did. "What business of it is yours?—You don't want me."

He didn't say anything. He just stood there and looked at me.

Feeling bolder because of the alcohol, I continued, "You

know I like you and all you do is treat me like a sister or something." My hands were on my hips now.

"Meet me outside—we need to talk," he told me, sounding like he was my father.

I was about to tell him off when Jonathan walked up. "Why are you telling my girl to meet you outside?"

Jaye looked at me. *"Your* girl?"

"He's just playing," I said.

"No, I'm not," Jonathan said. "What do you want with my date?"

"You mean your date that's about to end." Jaye's fists were balled up by his side.

Holding the drinks towards me so I could take them, Jonathan was up in Jaye's face. "Is that right?"

I didn't take the drinks. If I did, that would've freed Jonathan's hands, and Jaye looked like he was to ready to fight. I didn't want this to get blown all out of portion. I looked at my watch. "Jonathan, "I have to leave anyway."

"Well, I can take you home."

Jaye looked at me, pleading with his eyes.

"No, that's okay—Jaye will take me. You stay and enjoy the party. Call me tomorrow, and maybe we can get together again." Before he could respond, I took Jaye's hand and was out the door.

On the sidewalk, I looked at Jaye and said, "This better be good."

He pulled out a mint and handed it to me. "Your breath smells like alcohol."

"So?"

"I want to kiss you."

I couldn't get that mint in my mouth fast enough; as a matter of fact, I asked for two. That was the beginning of us.

We'd been together for so long, it's a given that we'd been through some drama. Once people in school realized that

Jaye was mine and I was his, the passes came regularly from both ends—the girls and the guys. It was like all of a sudden I was popular. The girls wanted to know what I had to snatch up the likes of Jaye, and the guys were just like, "Oh, she must be fuckin' now."

I even got into a fight or two over him. Now mind you, I didn't start them. Girls would just come up to me and start instigating, and I would go home upset, close to tears. My brothers, fed up with me being a punk, decided it was time for me to learn some self-defense. So, for a whole week after school, we would go downstairs in the basement and work on my boxing skills. As my skills improved, my confidence shot way up—I was looking for a fight and ready to kick some ass. "Next time someone get all up in my face, they're going to get it!" I declared.

It didn't take long for that to happen. One day after school this girl approached me at my locker and had the nerve to tell me she was going to take Jaye from me. I beat her so bad I got suspended. When I came back to school, no one bothered me.

When it came time for college, I grew depressed because I would be going away and Jaye was staying in the area. He chose to stay home and take care of his family. I knew things would change between us; I didn't believe in that absence-makes-the-heart-grow-fonder shit. In my mind, he was a man and a man needed sex. I wasn't going to be there to give it to him, so he would get it from somewhere else. Before I left, I told him, "Maybe we should see other people." I didn't think he'd say okay; I was just trying to protect myself. You know what?—his ass agreed.

"What do you mean, 'okay'?" I was hurt and angry.

"Why are you getting all upset?—you're the one who suggested it."

He was right. I'd played myself. I should have told him I changed my mind, but I felt like for him to say yes, it must have been something he was thinking about all along. So, off to college I went, and single I stayed.

Every guy I met I tried to measure up to Jaye—that wasn't kosher. I missed him so much; being young and in love, I thought I was going to die without him. Isn't it something . . . how when we're young, we go to the extremes? I was constantly wondering how and what he was doing. Little did I know, he was doing just fine—a whole hell of a lot better than me—which I found out from a phone call.

"Jaye is messing with some hoochie, and she's walking around talking about she's pregnant by him," Keke told me.

I was on my way home that weekend. You could imagine my heartache. A confrontation was in order.

"It's not my baby," Jaye insisted, the second he saw me. "Why can't Keke mind her business?"

"She's my best friend and she felt I had a right to know."

To make a long story short, we broke up. Baby momma drama—I wasn't having it. I was torn up inside and cried myself to sleep many nights. I even called up Kavan on the phone almost every day; I needed to understand, from a male's point of view, how Jaye could do this to me.

Kavan, tired of me being lonely, set me up on a date.

"I don't know," I told him.

"Well, I know—it's time for you to move on."

I knew he was right, so I went on a date with Mikal Robinson. He was going to college to be an attorney and looking for "wifey." We hit it off immediately.

Just as I was getting comfortable in this new relationship, Jaye found out, and all hell broke loose. He approached Mikal and told him to lay off, that I was his girl. They had a huge argument that almost turned into a fight. I told Jaye to stay away from me, and of course, he didn't listen.

Nine months later, the baby was born, and Jaye demanded a blood test; he thought the baby didn't look anything like him.

The mother kept putting it off, until finally he got smart and took her to court to have it done. As it turned out, he wasn't the father. The second he found out, he came crawling back to me, begging me to give him a second chance. At first I gave him a hard time, but he kept reminding me that I was the one who said, "Let's see other people." I still loved him and decided to give us another try.

"This is it"—I told him—"no more chances."

Young love
Innocent
Pain
Laughter and tears
Days
Months
Sometimes years

TIME TO SAY GOODBYE

Istepped out the shower, dried off, threw on a towel, and looked in the mirror. Today I decided to tell Jaye the news. When I walked into the bedroom, I noticed he'd fallen asleep. I stood over the bed and let my eyes roam down the length of his body, his skin the color of cocoa, his form that of a runner's, lean and tight. *He's so handsome.* Even after all these years, I was still attracted to him.

I reached over and touched his chest. "Jaye," I whispered in his ear, "we need to talk."

"About what?"

"I want to move."

"Move where?" He still wasn't all the way awake, so I knew he wasn't listening.

"California."

That got his attention. He opened his eyes and asked, "As in the West Coast?"

"I believe that's where California is located."

"When did this come about?"

"I've been thinking about it for quite some time."

"Why?"

"I want to pursue my writing career."

"Your writing career?"

I hated when he did that—repeat what I say with a question.

"That's what I said."

"Hmmm."

" 'Hmmm'? What does that mean?"

"Why can't you stay here and write? You've done it for this long." He sat up.

I knew he would say that.

I'd had quite a few articles in the local paper and in some magazines, such as *Essence, Heart & Soul,* and *Glamour.* To him, it was a big deal, and in a way it was. I knew there were thousands of writers out there who would've loved to see their work in print; I knew because I was one of them. The rejection slips were flowing steady. "Sorry, but we don't take unsolicited work; you need an agent."

Then the agents would say, "We're not taking on new writers."

It seemed like a lose-lose situation. So, to have my work published at all, to see my name in print anywhere, was still a big deal. It's just that I saw the bigger picture. I knew I could do better than have a few articles printed, because I'd been working on screenplays for the past five years and had just recently re-polished them. Now I was ready to go do my thing.

"When did you come up with this idea?"

"I've been thinking about it for a couple of years and—"

"You've been thinking of moving across the fuckin' country for a couple of years and you're now telling me this shit?"

"You need to take it down a notch," I told him.

Standing up and pacing the floor, he looked at me, started to say something and seemingly thought better of it.

"I really want to do this."

"What about us? Are we supposed to have one of those long-distance relationships or something?"

"I was hoping you would come out with me."

"How am I supposed to do that? Am I just supposed to up and leave my business on a whim and follow you? Is that what you were hoping?"

"Honestly, I don't know what I thought. I just know that this is something I need to do, and either you're going to be supportive or you're not. Either way, I'm going." *If looks could kill, I'd be dead.*

I didn't mean to sound like a bitch, I really didn't. But this was my life and my decision. I'd been waiting on this man to marry me for quite some time, and he kept putting it off. I was tired of waiting. Now, don't get me wrong, I couldn't imagine being without Jaye, but was I supposed to put my life on hold waiting for him? I saw women all the time, giving up their lives, losing themselves for men, and where did it leave them?—With a man, yes, but unhappy, unsatisfied, and depressed. I didn't want to go that route.

Obviously pissed, Jaye stood up and walked towards the bathroom. "I need to think. I'll call you later, and we'll discuss this further."

I stood up and followed him into the bathroom. "Jaye, I don't mean to sound harsh, but there's nothing to discuss. I love you, you know that, but I love me too and I want to follow my dreams. Of course, I want you to be there with me, supporting me, sharing in what I hope to be my success—our success—you should know that. It's just that we've been together for so long, since we were kids, and we're not married."

"Is that what this is about—marriage? I told you we would get married when the time is right financially."

"When is that? When you have a million dollars in the bank? How much or how little money you have shouldn't determine when we get married. The only thing that should determine that is us wanting to be together."

"Well, if it'll stop you from going to California, let's pick a wedding date."

I just looked at him. *That's the kind of shit that kills me, when a person will only step to the plate when under pressure.* Taking a deep breath, I told him, "Listen, let's just talk more about this later."

"Are you kicking me out?" he asked.

"No. Ten seconds ago, you said *you* were leaving; at least, that's my recollection. And I think it's a good idea, because I'm liable to say the wrong thing, and so are you."

He went into the bathroom and slammed the door. I waited until I heard the water running before I started crying. Wiping my tears, I told myself, "Be strong, you have to live your life for you."

I was in the kitchen preparing breakfast when I heard Jaye getting out the shower and preparing for his day. I waited for him to come eat, so we could talk a little more.

Instead, I heard him yell out, "I'll call you later," and the front door slammed behind him.

I can't believe he left like that. He didn't even give me a kiss goodbye. I picked up the phone to call Keke, my best friend. She'd listen to me drown in my sorrows.

It felt like she'd been my best friend forever. (She came into the neighborhood at the right time—when I was in serious need of a friend.) The only problem—she attended private school while I attended public. She'd just moved into the neighborhood, and I was eyeing her from my bedroom window, wondering what kind of toys she had. I was tired of playing with mine and didn't enjoy playing with my brothers much, so to see a little girl across the street . . . well, that was big.

My mother came into the room and saw me peeking out the window. "What are you looking at?"

"A little girl just moved across the street."

"Why don't you go introduce yourself?"

Excited, I grabbed my best doll and ran outside. By the

time I got across the street, they were in the house. I knocked on the door.

It swung open, and there she stood.

"Hi, I'm Layla. Want to be friends?"

"Okay."

It was that easy, and we'd been tight ever since. We were total opposites, I have to say. There were times when she got on my nerves. A bearer of bad news—that's what she was, at times. She would say, "I just keep it real." I loved her for that.

One of the things I loved most about Keke was she would try anything once. Maybe even twice, just to make sure she got it right the first time around. Me, I was more cautious and careful; I had to think it through for a while before even attempting something new. That was one of the reasons it took me so long to make this decision to move, and nothing and no one was going to stop me.

I knew she would support me in my decision. *That's what friends are for—to be there when you have nowhere else to turn.*

A friend indeed
A friend I need
To advise
To support
To listen
Without effort

JAYE

I just couldn't believe this shit. I felt l like I was being pushed in a corner, like my woman lost her mind, talking about moving all the way to California. Here I was, a good man, loving her since the 9th grade, and she just wanted to up and move. That's how little our relationship meant to her.

Yeah, yeah, we weren't married, but that didn't mean it was never going to happen. I just needed more time to get it together financially. I wanted to be able to give her a wedding in style. I wanted her to not have to work, to be able to chill, stay at home, and have our babies. Sexist? That's not how I'm trying to sound. I'm just saying it would be nice to give her the option of working or not. Old-fashioned? Yeah, I was.

My parents struggled. We were poor. There were three of us. My father couldn't keep a job. It's not like he didn't try because he did; it just seemed like luck wasn't on his side. He would tell all of us to have our own business, do whatever we had to do, so that we could be the boss. He didn't want us to struggle as adults and instilled in us a drive and a sense of pride.

The tragedy of it all was he committed suicide, leaving us all alone with my mother, who became depressed and forgot we existed. *Ain't that some shit?* He also left us all a letter, saying how much he loved us and wished he could have done right by us. As far as I'm concerned, the best thing he could have done to show that love was to stay around.

I didn't want my kids to want for anything. I wanted to be able to give them the world, to provide for them, love them and basically be able to retire and enjoy life with them. That's why I worked so damn hard; it was for the future. We all know the lyrics from the song "If This World Was Mine":

If this world was mine
I would place at your feet all that I own

I wanted to do that for Layla, but she was just impatient. I knew she loved writing. It was something she's always wanted to do and did. Hell, I was her biggest fan. Why didn't she know this? She wrote screenplays, but so did a lot of other people. I wasn't trying to shoot her down, but I was just being realistic. Didn't she realize how many people wanted to be famous, to be in the entertainment industry? Only few are chosen. Yeah, maybe she'd be one of those few, but then again, maybe not. Why couldn't she just stay in New Jersey and write, submit her work? Why did she have to move?

"You can come with me," she kept saying.

Yeah, right. I had a business here to run. I was just supposed to up and leave?—I don't think so. I'd worked hard for my business, EZ Compute Inc. We designed computer programs, repaired computers, and trained people on them. I was making decent money, and I had two guys working for me. Unbeknownst to everyone, I was probably going to be a millionaire in five years. *Maybe I should tell her this. Maybe that'll make her stay.*

Damn, why she got to go and do this to me. Maybe her mother will talk her out of it. I know her brothers won't; they spoiled her. They thought she could do it all. Not saying I don't, she just doesn't need to. Why couldn't I love a normal woman, one whose ambitions were maybe just a tad bit lower? A woman that woulda been happy with a regular job, doing regular things, and having a regular household. Then again, this could just be one of the reasons I loved Layla—because of her ambitions, her dreams and hopes. Lord knows she had enough of them for the both of us.

I even told her we could go ahead and get married. She acted like she was pissed. I didn't want to lose her. I really didn't.

"I know what to do—I'll go talk to her mom and plead my case. Maybe, just maybe, she'll side with me and together we could come up with a way to change Layla's mind."

I didn't want her to leave; I needed her here with me.

Please don't go
Stay
Where you belong
By my side
My equal
My life
My breath
My everything
My reason
Please don't go

IN NEED OF ADVICE

Ms. Hudson was sitting on the porch when Jaye pulled up. She smiled when she saw him and started to stand up to give him a hug.

"Don't get up," he told her and bent over to hug her. Jaye loved her like she was his birth mother. When his mom went into her depression after his father's death, she kind of took care of him and his siblings. She reminded him of Patti Labelle. She had that southern diva feel to her—dainty, lady-like, and full of pizzazz.

Jaye popped up every now and then, just to say hello, just never this early. She knew him like one of her own; she knew something was up. "What brings you by?"

"Have you spoken to your daughter this morning?"

Jaye knew Layla and her mom were close. He figured Layla would call her as soon as he left. If not her mother, then definitely Keke.

"No, why? Are you two arguing?" Ms. Hudson knew they'd been doing that a lot lately and Jaye always came running to her.

"Not exactly." Jaye was silent for a short moment, lost in his thoughts and Ms. Hudson just let him be. Finally looking up at her he said, "You know I love Layla, right?"

"Of course, sweetie. You two have loved each other for as long as I can remember."

"Well, it might be over."

Ms. Hudson sensed something was going on with Layla. The couple of times she'd stopped by in the last few days, she caught Layla staring off in space, deep in her own thoughts. So when Jaye said that, she just looked at him and waited for him to continue. She figured they'd been together for so long and still hadn't set a wedding date, so either it was going to go up or down.

When she didn't say anything, Jaye grew suspicious. "Well, what do have to think about that?"

"Well, sweetie, I'm not surprised. I could tell that Layla was getting restless; after all she did come from my womb."

"Well, how come I didn't recognize this?"

"You're a man, and sometimes some men don't pick up on what women are going through; we keep it hidden deep within ourselves."

Jaye just looked at her. This wasn't the conversation he had in mind—the "you're-a-man-and-you-wouldn't-understand" speech.

"I know you don't want to hear that, but it's a reality. You haven't even told me what happened and I already know that, whatever it was, my daughter was the initiator. Now am I wrong?"

"No, you're not. She's done put it in her mind that she needs to move to California to be a writer. Hell, she's already a writer."

Normally, Layla and her mother discussed everything, especially major decisions, so this news did come as a surprise to Ms. Hudson because Layla hadn't discussed this with her. Although it hurt to know her daughter was considering moving 3000 miles away, Ms. Hudson would support her. Hell, Layla's talent was obvious since she'd been little. As a matter of fact, a small part of her wondered what had taken Layla so long to make this move.

"You have to let her find her own way, Jaye. You can't be angry at her for wanting to move on and you can't stop her; you're not married—remember that."

"Why California?"

"Because that's where she wants to go."

"You're her mother—can't you stop her?"

"I can't do that; this is her life. She's grown, and not that you need a constant reminder, but you and her are not married, have no kids."

"I offered to marry her."

Ms. Hudson rolled her eyes.

"I did."

"When? Before or after she told you that she would like to move?"

Jaye grew quiet.

"I thought so."

"Ms. Hudson, you know that eventually we will get married."

"Well, I hate to be the one to tell you this—eventually isn't good enough."

"I don't know what else to do."

Taking his hand in hers, Ms. Hudson looked Jaye in the eyes and said, "Let me ask you this—why haven't you married her before now?"

"I was waiting for the right time."

"When would that have been?"

"When I had enough money saved to live a comfortable lifestyle."

Ms. Hudson knew what Jaye was doing. He was trying to make up for his father's suicide. "Baby, you and your father are two different people; you don't have to have riches in order to love."

Jaye knew she was right, but he would never admit it. Standing up, he told her, "I'm sorry I came over here with my problems, but I figured she's your daughter and you'd like to know that she's not only leaving me, but you and her brothers as well."

Knowing that this was his way of venting, she decided to let it pass and said, "Well, thanks for informing me."

Jaye looked at her and tried to think of something to say that would put her on his side. Nothing came, so he just hugged her and walked off the porch.

Ms. Hudson shook her head and walked in the house to call her daughter, whose phone was busy.

Children are born
From our wombs
We cherish them
Sometimes smothering them
Trying to keep them close
But the time comes
When they leave the nest
Branch out
And get a dose
Of life
On their own

YOUR HEART'S DESIRE

I'd just told Keke about my decision to move. I was springing it on everyone.

"Well, you've got to do what you feel in your heart," Keke told me.

"I know and I am."

"You'll call me later?"

"I will." When I hung up the phone with Keke, I stood by the window looking out and daydreaming. Like I said earlier, I loved Jaye, but it was time to move on.

You're probably thinking the only reason I was leaving was because we weren't married—that wasn't it. Well, not all of it, I just felt like it was time to do my thing, to follow my dreams, to pursue the greatness I know was out there for me. Especially in light of 9/11 and the sniper murders, where so many innocent lives were taken. I didn't want to be one of those "I should have, could have, if only I did" people.

What I needed to do was sit down and put together a final plan, now that I'd made the decision to move. Of course, I was scared as hell. What if I went out there and failed? What if nothing went according to plan? I needed to calm my ass down. I didn't need to talk myself out of this.

Maybe I'll go the gym and get my workout on, work off some of this tension and stress that's building. I was scared, nervous, and petrified, but I was also determined.

I stood in front of the mirror naked before putting on my gym gear. I took inventory of my body. I had to admit sometimes I was obsessed with how I looked. I could take my body apart; pick out all the flaws in less than one minute. Not saying I was obese, because I wasn't.

"Girl, most women would kill to have a body like yours," Keke would tell me.

Who was she to talk? We were the same way. Laughing out loud, I thought about her grabbing her knee talking about, "Look at the fat on my knees." Then she'd start walking around holding her knees. That shit was hilarious.

"The inner thigh, girl, the inner thigh." I grabbed the fat deposit that was visible to my eyes only. "If I were ever to get liposuction, this is where it would be." My measurements were 36-25-40, which basically meant I had a mouthful of breast, a small waist, and a black woman's ass.

Now when it came down to it, I knew what it was that kept those few extra pounds on me—sweets, plan and simple.

"You need to stop eating that shit," Keke would tell me while stuffing her face. "All that working out you do . . . I don't understand it."

Keke, now that was my girl. She was a pediatrician with her own practice. It was pretty ironic when I thought about it. The last year of high school she talked her mother into letting her attend public school with me. It wasn't a good move. She was disliked for no apparent reason other than her beauty and her smarts. Girls were always trying to jump her, and now the same haters trusted her with their kids.

I was a little jealous that she was doing what she always dreamed of. Me, I had to be the artistic one with the dream of a million others.

* * *

Pulling up into the gym, I grabbed my towel and head-phones out the backseat of my car and climbed out. When I entered the gym, I headed straight for the treadmills.

The first person I spotted was that hussy, Lynn. Who was Lynn? This wench was always trying to press up on Jaye. Now don't read me wrong, I wasn't turning away because of fear—I'd beat an ass if I had to—I was turning away because I had to step to her once. And of course she denied what I knew to be true. Ever since, she'd been trying to be my friend. I didn't need the bullshit, so I headed for the bikes instead. I threw my head-phones on and pedaled for an hour, getting lost in the sounds.

Sweaty and funky, I drove home to take a shower. After-wards, I'd planned on going to my mother's for dinner.

When I pulled into the parking lot, I was surprised to see my mother walking towards her car.

"Ma!" I rolled down my window and called out.

She turned around and smiled.

I parked the car and met her at the front door.

"This is a nice surprise," I told her while unlocking the door. "Actually, I planned on coming over in a couple of hours. Is everything okay?"

She followed me into the house. "Jaye came to see me today."

"Oh, he did?" This wasn't too much of a shock; he always ran to her when I did something he believed to be wrong.

"When did you plan on letting me and your brothers know about this big move? How do you plan to live? What are you going to do about a job? You know my feelings are hurt that you didn't even discuss this with me." She didn't give me a chance to answer the first question.

What could I say? I didn't discuss it with her for fear that she'd try and talk me out of it. I couldn't be mad at her for bum-rushing me.

"Ma, I can take care of myself. I've got money saved; I won't have to go to work immediately. I'll be staying with Kavan until I find an apartment."

* * *

Me and Kavan went way back. He was my second-best friend. Homeboy went to California to do his thing, which was comedy, and you know what, he succeeded in a big way. He'd been in movie after movie. Even opened his own comedy club. Large, he was definitely living.

We'd lost contact after he left Jersey. That was up until two years ago, when he came home to visit. "You still writing?" he asked one night while we were out to dinner.

"Never stopped," I told him.

"So what are you going to do about it?"

His question caught me off guard. "Huh?"

"I didn't stutter—I asked you, 'What are you going to do about it'?"

Seeing I had no answer, he went on to say, "Life is short, too short to waste your talent. We have wars going on, terrorist blowing shit up. I'm dying from AIDS, and here you have a gift that you're not even trying to pursue wholeheartedly. Don't waste what God has given you."

Needless to say, my mind was blown. "AIDS? Did you just say you have AIDS? What are you talking about?"

"Honey, this isn't about me, this is about you. I remember when we were young and all you talked about was writing, being a novelist, writing for the movies, for television—what happened?"

I still hadn't gotten past the AIDS part and he wanted me to talk about writing. "I'll answer you if you answer me."

He looked me in the eye. "I'm not dying, but I do have HIV. I've had it for years; it's not a big deal, it's something I'm learning to live with."

How could he act so nonchalant about it, like this was some shit you announced every day? "Do your parents know?"

"Of course, you know I can't keep secrets." Together we laughed.

We joked about the time when he told his parents he was

gay. It was on Thanksgiving Day and he was saying the prayer. He thanked God for the food, for his health, and for allowing him to have parents that would accept him as a gay man and wouldn't disown him.

"Remember that?" he asked.

"How could I forget? I not only choked on the turkey, but I thought your father was going to come across the table and kill you."

Shortly afterwards, Kavan dropped out of high school, got his GED, moved to California, and shocked everyone by becoming a star.

After a moment's silence, he told me, "It's funny how acceptance comes with money."

When Kavan left for California, it started me thinking about the direction my life was taking—*Am I fulfilled? Am I doing what I want to do or what I'm expected to do?*

I decided to make a plan and put it in action. Why? Well, what he said made a lot of sense. I had three choices—to be lazy, to be mediocre, or to excel. I had to admit I was being mediocre and too contented, accepting less than what I wanted in my life and my relationship. It was time to be active. After all, I had to create my own experience and circumstance. If I went out to L.A. and got rejected, I had to think of it this way—any rejection is God's protection.

Reach
Hope
Dream
Soar
Be It
Do It
Claim It
Now!!!!!!!

DINNER AT MOM'S

Now let me tell you a thing or two about my brothers. Justice and Ali were their names, and they were fine as hell. It was a shame we were related.

"So, you're leaving us for real?" Ali asked.

I didn't know why he was asking, because he was the first person I told when I started really considering it. Maybe he didn't believe me. Maybe he thought it was all talk. Actually, he was the first person I told a lot of things. He just listened most of the time, and that's just what I needed—someone to listen, not offer their opinion and tell me what I needed to do and how to do it.

Justice was the complete opposite—his way was the only way and the right way. Where Ali would listen; Justice would interrupt and try to get up all in my business; whether I wanted him to or not. Sometimes it irritated the hell out of me, yet at times I needed his aggressiveness.

"Yep, it's time for me to grow up and stop depending on my brothers," I told Ali, trying to make light of the situation. *Why was everyone bugging out, acting like we were never going to see one another again?*

"Maybe I should come with you to California, just to make sure you get settled."

"That's not necessary," I told him, although it made me feel good to know he would do something like that.

"You know I will—all you have to do is say the word."

Deciding to change the subject, I asked, "Where's Justice?"

Ali laughed. "Probably over some girl's house, you know your brother."

My brothers, I loved them like they came from my womb. Although overprotective and overbearing, they looked out for me when it came to life, money, and men.

Case in point, Jaye and I were going through a little something when we got back together after that whole pregnancy scare. I didn't trust him. I was always questioning him. "Where are you going? Who are you going with?" We'd have argument after argument. One time I smushed him in the face, and he pushed me away from him. I fell over the couch and hit my arm on the coffee table, bruising it.

I didn't care. "You will not put your hands on me in any way, shape or form." So, I called the police. They came to the house and tried to smooth things over with us. I didn't tell my brothers what happened because Justice would take a person out if he felt they did me some harm. I didn't want that. I was just trying to let Jaye know that he better not touch me again. Even if I did smush him, I was a girl; there was only so much damage I could do to him.

Well, one evening I was at the gym, and Ali was there. He saw the bruises and asked about them. Not thinking, I told him what happened. Next thing you know, he was at Jaye's office, informing him that if he ever put his hands on me again, he would end up hurt or dead. The incident was kept from Justice, because with him, there would be no talking.

Ali taking action was a surprise, because he normally thought everything through before acting out. He had a schedule that he adhered to. His palm pilot didn't just sit like mine. So, for him to offer to come and stay in California until I got settled . . . well, that was big. It meant that he would drop his orderly life and disrupt it to watch over me. Just the thought made me get up and give him a hug.

"What's that for?" he asked, while hugging me back.

"For being you."

Ali was a teacher. A cool teacher. At least that's what the kids said. He was the kind of teacher who, if you saw him sitting on his porch, would've invited you to join him. The kind of teacher that you could've talked to about sex and drugs; he was unconventional. The students trusted and respected him. They opened up to him and tried to do their best, knowing that's what he expected.

He was currently in a relationship with a female I couldn't stand—Tracy—a damn hoochie mama. You know the kind . . . with the fake hair, the fake nails, and tight clothes. I couldn't understand it—why would he be attracted to someone like that?

When I asked him, he said, "It's the inner, not the outer, that makes me stay."

Every time I saw them together, I wanted to kick her ass. It took a lot for me not to get ghetto on her, but it was his life and I couldn't control who he fell in love with.

As for my brother Justice—straight whore, straight playa— every time you turned around, he had a new woman. A new follower—that's what I liked to call them. For some reason, he could get them to do whatever he said. "Yes, Justice. Okay, Justice."

I found it sickening. Okay, he was fine, he did make a lot of money as a musician; he had an album out, but so what? He was still a man.

My mother was in the kitchen. She didn't sit down and eat with us like she normally did. I knew it was because I was moving. I glanced towards the kitchen and then at Ali. "Why is she staying in the kitchen?"

"You know why."

"Isn't that a little childish?"

"She's entitled; you're her only daughter and you're moving across the country."

Standing up, I took my plate off the table and walked into the kitchen. My mother was already washing the pots and pans from dinner, putting the food in Tupperware.

"You need my help?" I asked, hoping she would say no. I needed to go home and pack.

"No."

"Okay. Ali is still out there. I'm going home."

"Okay."

She was being very short with me. I knew why, but was getting irritated by it because when she was at my house earlier, she wasn't acting like this.

"I love you," I told her.

"I love you too," she said without looking up.

I stood there for a second or two, waiting for her to say something. When I caught on that she wasn't, I left; closing the door gently behind me.

I'm sorry
But I have to go
I don't expect you to understand it
But you need to know
It times for me
To move on
To leave the nest

I'M OUTTA HERE

I really thought I had one of the best jobs ever: being around books all day and having access to hundreds of authors. Who could ask for anything more? Oh, and my staff was the best, always on time and helpful. I didn't understand how people worked at jobs they hated, especially when a majority of their waking time was in that location. Forget that—I wasn't the one. A nine-to-five office job wasn't for me, and it wasn't because I didn't want to work. I just didn't want to be locked down to any one place for that long—I needed interaction, creativity.

This was the day I was to hand in my resignation. Honestly, I felt a little distressed about it. I'd been working here for so long that I knew most of the customers, started a writers' group, and hired just about all the part-timers. *A girl's gotta do what a girl's gotta do, and it's time to live life on my terms.*

"What's up, Layla?" Trina said.

She was my best worker. If I could pick the next assistant manager, she'd definitely be the one. Very dependable. "Nothing," I told her and kept walking. Normally I'd take the time out to talk with her, but not today. I had to resign now while I had the nerve.

Chris, the manager, was in the back doing inventory when I walked in.

"Can I talk to you for a minute?" I stood next to him as he looked at the clipboard.

"Sure." He continued counting.

"I'm leaving." I just thought I'd blurt it out, straight up.

Not really getting the gist of what I was saying, he asked, "Where are you going? What time will you be back? I have to leave early today." He was still counting.

"I'm going to California."

"Oh, have a nice time. When are you coming back?"

"I'm not."

Finally, he stopped counting and looked at me. "What?"

"Let's go into your office." I led the way without waiting for a reply.

When we entered the office, I smiled inwardly, thinking, *I'm going to miss this place.* I loved his space. When he wasn't at work, I sort of adopted it. He had it painted ocean blue, and his boyfriend, an artist, painted a bench on one wall and clouds on another, giving you the feel of the beach.

"You're not coming back?—Did I hear you correctly?"

"You heard right. I've decided to move West."

"What? Write?"

I nodded. Everyone who knew me knew that was my passion.

"When are you leaving? Do you have a place to live? Do you have a job set up?" Chris was acting worse than my mother; asking me question on top of question.

I patted him on the hand. "It'll be okay, sweetie. I'm on top of everything. I'm giving you one week's notice. I know you would appreciate two, but I have to leave while I've got the guts.

"I'll be staying with Kavan. I've saved up some money, so I won't have to work immediately."

"Well . . . I see you have this all planned out."

"I do." If I didn't know any better, I'd say that Chris looked hurt.

"I don't want to lose you; you've done so much for this store. I'll miss you, your workers will, and the customers will. You know we have a branch in L.A. If you wanted to work there, all you have to do is say the word."

I stood up and went over to Chris. "Stand up."

He did.

I gave him a big hug and a peck on the lips. "I'll miss you. You know that, don't you? You're one special white boy."

He took my hand while laughing, and together we walked towards the door. "Let's go let the crew know."

It felt good to know I was going to be missed. *So often we go through this life not realizing our worth or the fact that we touch people.*

Work was tough that day. Not from labor, but because I knew it would be a while before I saw these people again, if ever.

That evening when I arrived home I called Jaye, but there wasn't any answer. So I called Keke instead and told her to meet me at Reddy's for a drink. (Reddy's was a local bar; the place everyone went when they wanted to be seen.)

Now the last thing I wanted was to be seen, but I figured, *what the heck . . . might as well get out, do the community bar thing. Never know who I might run into, considering I didn't plan on coming back any time soon.* Little did I know it would turn into an emotional scene.

Keke was cracking up. "You mean to tell me that he had the audacity to propose?"

"If that's what you want to call it."

Sensing I was more upset about it than I let on, Keke snapped, "The nerve of him."

"I know, right?"

The next thing you know, I was boohoo crying. Not only did this shock me, but it shocked the shit out of Keke as well.

"Wait—why are you crying? What's that about? Are you ready to leave? You want to go to the ladies' room?"

Keke couldn't get her words out fast enough. She looked like she was about to cry right along with me, but I knew she wouldn't—it would mess up her makeup.

Keke was one fly sister. Skin, the color of chocolate, and eyes, the color of caramel, she always had it together. She wore her hair bone-straight—it was never out of place—make-up impeccable, and designer gear only. Not because she was materialistic, but because she could afford it.

I went from crying to laughing in less than a minute. "I think I had too much to drink," I told her. "I'm an emotional wreck."

She said nothing.

"You know, I really love that man and have for a long time, with his faults and all. Ever since I met him, when I first saw him in school, I wanted to marry him. I've waited and waited. And it's been one excuse after another—'Wait until this.' 'Wait until that.' What the hell are we waiting for?—the perfect moment. There is no perfect moment. Well, you know what, I'm tired of waiting. What does he think I am?—No, what does he think I'm going to do?—Sit around and wait for the rest of my life? Well, I'm not; I'm out of here. Am I not good enough to marry? Is that it? Is he waiting just in case someone better comes along? Is he trying to have his cake and eat it too? God, I hope I'm doing the right thing and not just playing myself."

Keke just listened to what I had to say.

I know there was a lot she wanted to say in return, but being the true friend she was, she chose to stay silent. Taking a deep breath, I told her I was done, said all I needed to say, and was ready to go home and get under the bed.

Keke put her hands in mine. "Girl, I think you're doing the right thing. You are so talented. I was wondering when you were going to wake up and be you; wake up and do you. I've got your back—believe that shit. Hell, believe in yourself because, if you don't, no one else will."

She said it with so much conviction. I joked and told her she needed to be a motivational speaker.

"I'm just saying—do what's best for you."

See now, that's the shit I'm talking about—a friend that knows what to say and when to say it, someone that will back your ass up, regardless. When you find a friend like that, you better keep them around because it's rare. People are so phony nowadays, looking out for self, wanting to be around you when you're down so that they can feel superior. Yep, been there, done that. Had those kind of friends. You know the ones I'm talking about—the kind that will drain you dry, the kind that by the time you get off the phone with them, you're depressed. I called them "energy vapors."

"Come on, girl, let's go." Keke said, breaking my train of thought. "Let's get you home."

"I can drive," I told her; already knowing she wouldn't let me. I'd had one drink too many.

"Not going to happen. I'll take you home, and we'll come pick up your car tomorrow."

When we pulled up to my place, Keke turned off the ignition.

I told her, "You don't have to come in. I'm okay. I just want to lay down and get some rest."

"You can lay down with me there; I won't bother you."

I gave her a kiss on the cheek. "I love you too, but I want to be alone right now."

"Are you sure?"

"Yes, I'm sure."

"Okay. Call me in the morning so we can go get your car."

"I will." I turned and walked away, knowing she would wait until I went inside before driving away.

When I walked into my apartment, a light flicked on, scaring the hell out me. I was about to scream until I saw that it was Jaye sitting on the couch.

"Where the hell have you been?"

"Out." I went into my bedroom.

He followed me. "With who?"

I felt like being a bitch. "Don't worry about it."

He sat on the bed.

I put my hands on my hips. "What? What do you want? Why are you here?"

"I want to spend some time with you before you leave."

"Oh, so now you're okay with the fact that I'm leaving." I sat on the bed next to him.

"No, I'm not okay with it, but if that's what you want to do, who am I to stop you?"

"Yeah, you're definitely not my husband," I said, just to be spiteful.

"I know that's why you're moving."

"It's not the main reason, although it does factor into it a little."

"We will get married when the time is right."

I stood up. "Jaye, please let's not go there. The time is never right—I'm tired of hearing that bullshit, okay? We had what we had."

"Had? Are you saying that we're over?"

I started pacing. "I'm saying that I can't see us having a long-distance relationship. You know, like I know, that it won't work. Remember what happened when I went to college?"

"That was a long time ago."

"I know, but still . . ."

"I love you, Layla."

"I know that too, but it's not enough for me. I want more

than love, I want to be married, and you obviously don't. I don't want to be asked just because I'm moving away either."

He said nothing.

"Can you leave now?"

"I want to stay."

I wanted him to stay as well, but I needed to clear my head. "Please, just go."

He stood up and looked me in the eye. "Please don't do this."

I almost broke down right then and there. If my phone didn't ring, who knows what I would have said and done? I picked up the phone. "Hello."

"What's up, sis?"

I put my hand over the mouthpiece and told Jaye, "I'll talk to you tomorrow."

"Who the hell is that calling here this time of the night?"

I rolled my eyes. "It's Justice."

He looked at me in disbelief and walked out the door.

I uncovered the phone and started crying.

"Layla, are you okay? Are you crying? You want me to come over there?"

Wiping my tears and sniffling, I told him, "That's not necessary." I looked at the clock. "Do you know what time it is?"

"Yeah, I can tell time. I went to Reddy's, and my boys said you had just left and you looked upset. I wanted to call and check on my baby sis."

"I'm all right."

"You don't sound it. Listen, how about we have lunch together tomorrow and we can talk?"

"You mean to tell me you're going to take time out of your busy schedule for me?"

"Yes."

"Okay. I have to teach kickboxing in the morning, so pick me up at one, my house."

"All right. I love you."

"I love you too."

After the call, I collapsed on the bed and closed my eyes, trying to envision my success; instead, my head started pounding.

One drop
Two drop
Three drop
Four
Someone's knocking
I refuse to answer the door
They're the tears
That fall
The heart
That breaks
How much more
Of this can I take

TIME TO SAY GOODBYE

The day of my departure had finally come. From the time I'd made my announcement until this day had been quite an adventure.

Jaye was blowing hot and cold—loving and hateful, bitter and sweet. Keke called me every day to talk about nothing.

My brothers took me out to dinner, and my mom . . . well, she was acting distant. I had to remind her that she was the one who taught us to take chances; to not be afraid.

The night before my scheduled flight, Jaye stayed over at my house, and I have to tell you, it was up there at the top of the list for romance. Homeboy went all out.

The bookstore gave me a going-away party, which was off the hook.

I was dead tired. I opened the door with one thing on my mind, and that was rest. Imagine my surprise to find a path of rose petals greeting me at the door. I followed them down the hallway into the living room, where candles were flickering everywhere and the fireplace was lit. The room smelled sexy and soft. My hands came up to my mouth, and tears welled in my eyes. I had no idea he would be doing this. If anything, I thought we were going to part on bad terms, especially since we'd had an argument earlier about me going to the party.

"I thought I'd surprise you and show you how much I'm going to miss you," Jaye said.

I was at a loss for words. All I could do was walk into his arms and place my lips on his. "Make love to me now," I told him.

He took my hand and led me into the bedroom. We sat on the bed facing one another, and he just stared at me.

"Why are you looking at me like that?"

"Because you're so beautiful and sometimes I forget."

For the first time in a long time, I could feel heat pulsating through my body. I hadn't experienced this sensation in a long time. The lovemaking, although good, had become routine.

Jaye lay back on the bed, and I stood up and undressed. Between my legs was moist with anticipation; I wanted him inside me immediately. I didn't want to wait for the foreplay; I wanted to be filled up.

"Sit on my face."

"I want you inside me first." I unbuckled his belt and pulled down his pants. When I finally had them all the way off, I climbed on top of him and slid down his shaft. I moaned from a place that I thought was lost. "You feel so damn good." I wanted him everywhere and in every position.

The lovemaking that night was intense. I gave him a place that I only let him enter a couple of times a year. Instead of concentrating on the pain, I thought about the pleasure it gave him. At one point he seemed to lose all self-control. It got to the point where I had to tell him, "Slow it down; you're hurting me."

When it was over, he held me so tight it felt like we were Siamese twins. I knew it was his way of saying he didn't want me to leave.

The next morning, every time I tried to move away from him, even if I was just turning over, he would pull me back.

Finally I said, "Jaye, I have to get up and finish packing."

He tried to act like he didn't hear me, so I repeated my self.

He looked at me. "So you're really leaving?" He sat on the bed and put his face in his hands.

"Excuse me." I reached over him for my robe, but he didn't move. "I said 'Excuse me.' "

He moved over slightly. "You're doing this to teach me a lesson?"

"What are you talking about? What kind of lesson you think I'm trying to teach you?"

"This has nothing to do with your dream, your destiny, this has to do with the fact that I waited too long to ask you to marry me. You feel like I used you or something."

I decided to kick his ass out right then and there. "Leave," I told him, point-blank.

"What?"

"You heard me—leave. I'm tired of having this same conversation. I would like to finish packing in peace."

"You're really kicking me out?"

"I'm not kicking you out; you're the one who said you wanted to leave."

"Layla, don't do this to me. Don't do this to us."

"Jaye, I'm not doing anything to anyone. I'm doing this for *me.*"

He stood up, pulled his pants, and grabbed his shirt without saying a word and walked out the door, slamming it behind him.

JAYE

She actually kicked me out . . . on the day she was leaving, no less. *Can you believe this shit?* I'd been thinking about our situation, our relationship, a lot this past week. I'd loved her for as long as I could remember. *How could she do this to me?— just up and announce she's leaving.* Okay, I should have stepped to the plate a long time ago, but I was scared. That's right, I said scared, but I'd rather be with her than without her. Couldn't she see that?

I went all out and planned a romantic evening, trying to show her what she'd be missing. Maybe it was too late, but still the effort was there. I loved the girl, and she was doing me "dirty."

Okay, okay, maybe I did wait a little too long to propose, but I'm a man. And I thought what we had was good. Guess I thought wrong. I just never thought it would come to this. *Maybe I should call Kavan and plead my case to him. He's a gentle spirit, willing to listen to both sides; maybe I can convince him. You know what, I'm not even going to go there because there is no way in hell he'll side with me.* And I know there was no way in the world I could go to Keke—she's never cared that much for me.

My girl was leaving me, and there wasn't a damn thing I could do about it.

Saying bye is hard to do
What is in the future
Lonely nights
Unbearable days
Insincere hugs
An unpassionate kiss
Saying bye
Being missed

SAYING BYE-BYE

My mother and my brothers chose to see me off, insisting on driving me to the airport. I hated goodbyes, so of course I tried to talk them out of it.

"I'm not hearing it," my mother said. "My baby girl is moving 3000 miles away and I don't go to the airport with her? Now what would that look like?"

We were all seated, waiting for my flight to be called.

"You have money?" Justice asked.

"Yes."

"Are you going to be okay out there by yourself?" Ali asked.

"Yes."

"Make sure you call home every week," my mother said.

"If you need us to come out there for any reason at all," Ali said, "just call us."

"Don't go out there talking to any knuckleheads," Justice added.

I just looked at him and rolled my eyes. I know they meant well, but all this fussing almost made me change my mind about going.

"Flight 56, first-class fliers, please line up."

That was me—first-class—leaving in style. Of course I didn't pay the extra cost; my brothers did. They insisted, saying I had to leave in style.

I stood up to hug my mom and brothers and heard Keke's voice yelling, "Wait! Wait!"

I looked down the corridor. She and Jaye were running down the walkway. I was surprised that they came together and that Jaye came at all.

Jaye stood off to the side, while Keke gave me a hug and said, "I'm going to miss you, girl. I love you, and I will come visit."

"I'm going to miss you too."

Jaye stepped up and held his arms out and I stepped into them. "I love you," he whispered in my ear, holding me tight.

"You should have married her then," Justice told him.

I looked over Jaye's shoulder and mouthed for him to shut up. I was about to apologize for Justice and his big mouth.

Jaye looked at Justice and held my hand. "You're right—I should have."

After giving everyone final hugs and kisses, I left them standing there and walked onto the plane. I took my seat and was ready to start my new life.

New beginnings
Full of adventure
Full of growth
Full of success
Doing my best
Achieving
Aspiring
To be more
To be true
To self
Looking after me
No one else

MY ARRIVAL

When I stepped off the plane, it was like entering the unknown. The six-hour flight was peaceful and serene. I had a window seat, which I always requested because I loved looking at the clouds. I always expected to see angels walking around. Leaving the peacefulness of the heavens and returning to the chaotic scene in the airport frightened me just a bit. I was scared as hell. I almost turned around and got back on the next flight back to Jersey. Had it not been for the sunshine and the excitement of seeing Kavan, I would have. After all in Jersey, it was winter time, which meant it was cold as hell, and I didn't feel like going through another winter.

As I made my way to the information desk, I tried not to look like a tourist. Then I reminded myself that I wasn't in New Jersey, but sunny California, and heck, everybody is a tourist at one point or another.

"Excuse me, but can you tell me where to get a taxi?"

I thought I would surprise Kavan by going a day earlier than planned. Knowing him, he'd go all out and have a limo pick me up.

Last time I spoke with him, he told me he was doing okay with having HIV. It's funny how when AIDS and HIV first came about, everyone was terrified. They didn't want to be around people who had it, scared to touch them or even breathe the same air as someone affected. Now it's sad to say that it's turned into such a common disease. The infected had learned to live with it and so did family and friends. When I really thought about it, maybe it was a good thing, because the fear is now gone. Maybe not one hundred percent, but something is better than nothing. It wasn't like it was a plague anymore. Another thing, I loved Kavan. That was my boy, and if he was dealing with it, then so could I.

I gave the taxi driver the address and requested that he take me the scenic route. Palm trees were everywhere. That was wild to me because although I saw it on television and in the movies, it was still a shock when I saw it in real life. They were even in the ghetto, or what I perceived to be the ghetto, which was basically apartment complexes cramped together so close, you could smell what your neighbor was cooking and hear the conversation clear enough to join in.

It was people not caring and hanging on the corners, appearing as if they didn't give a damn. I was actually seeing this out here. Which really surprised me, because when I thought of Hollywood, I thought of where the stars lived and of money growing on trees.

I thought it was tranquility and beauty everywhere, but that wasn't the case. Some of the streets the driver took me down were poverty-stricken. Another thing that surprised me was the mixture of people, the different races—Black, White, Puerto Rican, you name it. There also appeared to be a lot of same-sex and interracial couples.

Eventually, we pulled into a neighborhood that looked like money. I started to relax. For a second there, I was worried that Kavan was living "foul." I mean, I knew he had dough and all, but was it dough by Hollywood standards?

"We're here," the cabdriver said, pulling into one of the longest driveways I'd ever seen.

Damn, I thought as we got closer to the house, *if this isn't dough by Hollywood standards, it's definitely dough by Jersey standards, especially Branch Park.*

Kavan was living in a mansion and was holding out on a sister. *He didn't tell me about all this; he was being modest.* I was smiling from ear to ear, feeling proud as hell. Homeboy had done it. Came out here and did his thing—he was definitely representing for Jersey. I looked in awe at the house. Windows were everywhere, and you could almost see right into it.

"Would you like to pay me now?"

I laughed because I had yet to get out the car. I was too busy admiring the house. As I unlocked the door, I saw a limo pull up into the driveway. Not waiting for the driver to open the door, Kavan got out the passenger side and peered at the taxi, trying to see who was in it.

Stepping out the cab, I smiled, happy as hell to see him. "What? You forgot a sister was coming?"

He was just as happy to see me. We rushed into each other's arms.

"Oh shit, I can't believe you're here, and early at that."

Clearing his throat, the driver had his hand out waiting to get paid. I handed him the money as he gawked at Kavan. It was obvious he knew he was famous.

"You can leave now," I told him.

Without taking his eyes off Kavan, he put the money in his pocket and asked Kavan for his autograph. Which he gladly gave.

"Check you out—the movie star, signing autographs."

"It comes with success; you'll see when you have it."

I took his hands and tried to pull him along. I was dying to see the inside of his house.

Glancing around, Kavan asked, "Where are your bags?"

"The airport will be sending them via service."

"We'll send someone to pick them up."

"Cool."

"Come on in; take a look at my crib."

We walked in, hand in hand.

I have to tell you, his place was off the hook. It was all that and more—wall-to-wall, off glacier-white, plush carpet. I took off my shoes and sank my toes into it. "I guess you don't have company much. How do you keep your carpet looking like this?"

"Girl, it's called a cleaning service." Together we laughed.

You know how most houses are basic—living room, dining room, kitchen, bathroom, and bedrooms. Kavan had living room, dining room, game room, chill-out room with the big-screen TV and a serious radio system, a huge eat-in kitchen, three bathrooms, and three bedrooms all to himself. It was ridiculous.

If I had the money, I'd do the same.

"Let me show you my favorite place in the house."

I followed him to the backyard, and he pushed back the sliding doors.

"Or should I say outside the house."

He had an actual waterfall. "This is my spot for writing," I found myself announcing. Standing there, I could actually picture myself—incense burning, Horace Brown playing in the background, a glass of wine, chillin', the words flowing on paper.

I followed him back into the house. "I'm so proud of you." I gave him a hug. "I want to live just like you when I grow up." It may have sounded like a joke, but I meant every word. He'd followed his dream and was inspiring me to do the same.

After the tour of the house, we sat down to do some catching up. I told him how everyone was acting, with me leaving. "You would think they were never going to see me again."

"Girl, don't sweat it; it'll be okay. You just stepped out of the box they put you in and they don't know how to handle it. They'll get over it, don't stress yourself. What's done is done. You're here with me now."

Finally, the breakdown came, and Kavan wrapped his arms around me and held me tight. He wiped the tears off my face and kissed me on the cheeks.

Trying to lighten up the moment, I asked him about his love life.

Too blessed
No need to be stressed
All these tests
Trying me
Pushing me
To the limit
Don't lose sight
Its coming
The light
Of purity

KAVAN SPEAKS

Let me tell you about my love life. I'm sure Layla told you that I was gay. His name is TC Black. What a name! Hell, what a man! Sexy, chocolate brother wanted by men and women, had by men and women. All mine now ... well, as much as he can be.

He was in the closet, meaning no one knew he was gay, and from appearance you couldn't tell. A straight-from-the-video, roughneck type. He was a well-known producer in the music industry and was afraid if word got out he would lose his clientele, which consisted mostly of rappers. At least that's what he told me. I was sick of hearing it though. I didn't know how much longer I could go on with this "hiding us" shit. I felt like I was being played.

I couldn't be too choosy. I was HIV-positive and he knew. Safe sex when there was sex was the only way. For me, it was more about companionship.

Layla and I went way back. Actually she was the first and only girl I'd ever loved. I had the biggest crush on her growing up—her and the whole football team, that is. I'd been attracted to the same sex for as long as I could remember. I was too scared to tell anyone because, back in the day, people were vicious. That's why I had to leave that small-ass town. I

wanted to live my life out in the open, I didn't want to be looking over my shoulder every minute, wondering if people
knew, and how they would react once they found out.

Layla was the first person I told, and she was like, "So who
gives a fuck?"

I loved her so much and would've done anything for her,
and I believed she felt the same way.

As far as Jaye was concerned, I wasn't a fan of his because
my girl should've had a ring on her finger by now. Either that
or she should have been left Jersey. I was glad she'd finally
come to her senses. I'd been asking her to come for quite
some time, knowing she was wasting away in Jersey. Now don't
get me wrong, I would never disrespect where I come from,
that wasn't my style. I loved my hometown. It was just that the
opportunities were here, and I thought she should try and
take advantage of it. They say the only time a person fails is
when they don't try. She needed to at least make an effort. I
made one, and now I was rich as hell. It wasn't all about the
money, but it helped, let me tell you.

I always knew I was going to be a star. I once heard it said
that it's better to be a failure at something you love than a success at something you hate. Thankfully, I was doing what I
loved and was succeeding at it.

Success means different things
Numerous scenes
Money
Class
Style
Sex
Good livin'
Plenty givin'

I WANT TO GO HOME

This wasn't as easy as I thought it would be. I was here a few weeks and it seemed like six months. First of all, I was lonely as hell. I missed my family, my friends, the bookstore. I missed the familiar. I didn't know how much I counted and depended on my family until now. I honestly thought I could handle being 3000 miles away on my own, by myself. Little did I know, it would be a struggle. On top of everything else, I was horny as hell.

Now I have to keep it real and tell you that was one thing I knew I was going to miss—the dick. I thought I could go without it, but I was struggling. Me and celibacy didn't get along.

I had two options. The first was to find me a man, someone I could kick it and be intimate with, minus a commitment. Hell, when you think about it that should've been easy. It was the perfect arrangement for a man—free pussy, but the more I thought about it, the less attractive the idea seemed. There were too many diseases out there. Shit, there were probably some we didn't even know about. Not only that, I didn't want to hook up with the wrong brother and get myself a maniac, a stalker. Now that would've been some shit.

The other option was a toy. Yep, that's right, a vibrator. And

I had the chance to get one tonight at this thing called a pleasure party, a "fuckaware" party, as Kavan kept calling it. It was being hosted by a bunch of gay men. You know my ass let Kavan talk me into attending the affair.

Heck! I missed my family, I missed Keke, and I missed Jaye. I missed the sex, the bookstore—I missed it all. I was "PMSing" right now, and that's when I got the horniest.

I'd always wanted to be buck wild. I'd always wanted to just do my thing and not have to look over my shoulder, around the corner, or behind my back. Well, now this was my chance.

Honestly, I didn't think I was ready for a rebound lover yet.

"Girl, are you ready yet?" Kavan yelled from downstairs.

"I'm coming. Just need another minute or two." I looked in the mirror and smiled, liking what I saw. I pulled out my MAC lip gloss, put it on, smacked my lips together, and blew myself a kiss. I then dapped a little Blue Nile body oil on and went to meet Kavan downstairs.

Kavan was so sweet. Almost the perfect roommate. If I had to pick from a number of people who I wanted to live with, he would be the one, hands down. I'm sure you've heard horror stories about rooming with people. How either they were dirty, didn't like to clean up, inconsistent, pain in the asses, or roomies that were the complete opposite—anal retentive, where if you moved something a little to the left they would know. Well, none of those descriptions applied to Kavan.

He was so attentive when he was around, which he rarely was, that I had to remind him I was an adult and that I could take care of myself. I know it was his way of making me comfortable.

He was in the house most of the day and out most of the night. That's what being in show business was about. I don't know how he did it. He'd come home around four in the morning and still be wide-awake by ten, six hours later.

* * *

When we pulled up to the Hilton, I asked Kavan, "Why are we here?"

"Timothy, the host, rented out a suite."

We didn't even stop at the customer service booth, just headed straight for the elevator.

"I take it you know where you're going?"

"You take it right, honey," he said with a smile. "Be prepared for an awesome time."

Awesome was too weak a word for what I attended. More like *freaky deaky*. It was off the hook. I don't think I'd seen so many sex toys, lubricants, and books in my life. They discussed every sexual act you could think of and what you could do and use to enhance your sex life. It went from pleasure balm—a cream that not only made the penis stay erect longer, but if you swallowed some, it numbed your throat and you'd be able to give head all night long. (You know all Kavan's friends purchased that item.)—to the Mercedes of vibrators; at least that's how it was described. You know what? I purchased one called "the rabbit." The consultant got me for sixty dollars. *This shit better make me scream somebody's name.* I laughed at myself, wondering if I was that hard up. "I hope this toy works," I said to myself. Because a sister needed a release, on the real tip—I was that backed up.

"Did you have a good time?" Kavan asked when we arrived home.

"You know I did. I feel like I just left the school of hoochies, ho's, and homosexuals."

Kavan laughed. "You did."

That night I lay in my bed, letting my thoughts wander and take me down the road of self-pleasure. It'd been a long time since I masturbated and, like riding a bicycle, I didn't forget how to do it.

A night of pleasure
All alone
Touching my treasure
Finding my throne
A moan
Escapes me
Can't hold it back
I shudder violently
Wondering if it's all intact
My juices start to flow
Want to do it again
Gotta go

MAKING FRIENDS

When I arrived to teach a kickboxing class in a gym in downtown L.A. and I saw that the women participating were in better shape than me, I knew I was in trouble. Their bodies were a little thin but toned. So I immediately decided to bring it up a notch. Forty-five minutes into the class, I was sweating profusely. I didn't think I'd be that tired, but after not teaching in over a month, I should have at least expected it. After class, a few people came up to me and complimented me on the lesson.

I was wiping the sweat off my forehead, when a fine brother walks over. His complexion was a tad lighter than caramel. His eyelashes were long and curly, and he was bow-legged. He had thick muscular legs and was well groomed.

Something had to be wrong. His breath had to stink or something. There was no way a brother could be this fine and not have some type of flaw. I almost considered speaking first, but I didn't want to play myself. Normally, I was attracted to a darker-complexioned man, but he also reeked of power, and that shit was turning me on.

"Hello. You're new here?" he asked in a deep baritone voice.

"Yes."

"Where are you from?"

I almost said, "Where do you want me to be from?" but caught myself. "I'm a Jersey girl."

He laughed. "I thought so; I could hear your accent."

"Oh, really? Have you ever been to Jersey?"

"Yes. I'm from Brooklyn originally."

I looked at him again. Although handsome, he wasn't a pretty boy, but he didn't have that rugged look that most men from Brooklyn possessed either.

"You're talking about accents? Listen to yours."

"I'm proud of my Brooklyn roots, accent and all. Where are you off to?"

"I don't think that's any of your business."

"Yeah, you're definitely from Jersey, with the smart comebacks. Can I take you out to dinner or something?"

"No."

"Why not?"

"I don't even know you."

"We can get to know one another over dinner, Ms. Layla."

"You weren't in my class, how do know my name?"

"I asked one of your class participants."

"Oh."

"So how about it?"

I wasn't sure if I liked the aggressive type. "I'll think about it. I'll let you know next time I see you." I moved around him and walked out the room with him following me.

"Well, don't you wanna at least know my name?"

It would have been real mean if I'd said no, but I didn't. I have to admit, I was a little curious. "Yes."

"It's Wesley. Wesley Jones." He said it like I was supposed to know who he was.

"Okay." I walked away and into a woman who took my class.

"Your name is Layla, right?" She grabbed my arm.

"Yes." *What was this? Everyone was asking who I am.* I looked down at my arm and back at her, hoping she got the message to let the hell go.

"I liked your class."

"Thanks."

"I'm Quassmirah." She stuck her hand out for me to shake it.

"Nice meeting you."

"Do you know who that was just trying to press up on you?"

"He said his name was Wesley Jones."

"Yeah, but do you know who he is?"

From the excitement in her voice, I knew he had to be someone famous. I took the bait. I didn't feel like playing the name game. I wanted to go home and write, not stand here and talk about a man. "Who is he?"

"He the hottest producer in L.A. right now—the hottest, the finest, and the richest."

Then why don't you go after him? "That's nice."

"Did he ask you out?"

"Is everyone here so forward?"

She laughed my question off like I was joking.

"Let's go have a shake or something?"

"Maybe another time. I've got somewhere to be," I told her, wondering why she was trying to befriend me.

"All right. Then I'll check you later."

I watched her walk away. Her hips were swaying left and right. She was definitely Hollywood attractive, silky straight hair down her back, with streaks of blond in it. For all I know, it could've been a weave. Either she had on contacts, or her eyes were hazel brown. She also walked with a serious switch. I shook my head. Everyone here had that "I-want-to-be-a-star" look.

I went into the locker room to get my things and thought about a piece of advice Kavan had given me about the people in L.A. "Be careful who you befriend," he said. "Everybody wants something from someone, and don't believe words—make a person show and prove."

What is it that you want
My friendship or my soul
Will it add on to my life
Make me whole
Or will it break me down
Tear me apart
What is it that you want
My body
Or my heart

FEELS LIKE THE FIRST DAY OF SCHOOL

I was on my way to Wal-Mart to pick up a few school supplies for a screenwriting workshop.

Kavan had taken me sightseeing, to parties and various Industry events. I was having the time of my life, but I was also feeling stagnant, like I was freeloading. I couldn't have that.

I was anxious about school and about pursuing my dream. In Jersey, I was talented. In California, everyone and their mother were talented. So I know I had to stand out in some way, shape, or form. I kept hearing, "It's not how good you are, but who you know." Thank God I knew Kavan. *Perhaps when the time is right, he'll hook a sister up.*

I walked into Wal-Mart and started tripping because even the cashiers were beautiful.

I didn't have much else to do for the rest of the day and decided to go home and call Keke, try and convince her to come visit and perhaps hit the beach.

When I arrived home, Kavan was sitting on the couch with TC, his man of the moment. I knew it was him because Kavan said he was tall and dark, and this brother most definitely was.

"Layla, this is TC; TC, this is Layla."

TC stood up, all 6'-4" of him, and gave me a hug. "What's up?"

Now if a sister saw this man on the streets, she would not suspect he was gay. Not even a little bit. His stance, his voice, his mannerism reeked of masculinity. I couldn't help wondering who turned him out.

"Nothing. Just a little tired. Been running all day."

"You want to watch this movie with us?" Kavan asked.

"Nah, I just want to get in the Jacuzzi and chill, but first I'm going to call Keke."

"Well, I'll be up later."

I bent over and gave him a kiss on the cheek and told TC, "Nice meeting you."

Upstairs in my room, I lay across the bed and thought about my family. The last time I spoke to mama, she told me that Justice had another girlfriend, and that Ali was being considered for principal. She told me that she'd met a man and was considering letting him take her out. *What a surprise!* I was happy for her, but I knew my brothers wouldn't be.

"Has Justice and Ali met him?"

She laughed. "Are you serious?—they would have a fit."

She was right. They thought mommy belonged to no one other than them and our father. She spoiled them rotten; trying to make up for the fact dad was no longer around.

When he died she went into a depression, operated like she was programmed, went through the motions, fed us, bathed us, took us to school, and picked us up. No family outings, no activities. Life was one big uneventful time.

This lasted for a year, and suddenly one day we came home from school and she announced that we were going to the circus. We all looked at her like she'd lost her mind. Of course we wanted to go, but we didn't know where this was coming from. We had such a good time that day. We laughed, held hands, and ran wild. That night we climbed into the bed with her, all three of us. As we lay there thinking about our day, I found myself asking her how she and our father met.

She laughed. "Your father drove a milk truck."

All we ever knew of my dad doing was working for UPS.

"He did what?" my brothers asked, thinking this was the funniest thing they'd heard.

"That's so country," Justice said.

"Well," Mom laughed, "we're from the country."

The sound of mom's laughter was something I hadn't heard in quite some time.

"Growing up in Virginia, that was considered a lucrative job." She went on, "He would drive by my house every day. Me and my girlfriends would be sitting on the porch, playing jacks, laughing and talking about boys. One day we were on the porch and Kristie said, 'You know Randall?—the guy that drives the milk truck—whenever he passes by he looks at you.'

"I told her she didn't know what she was talking about. See, I was pretty, but not the prettiest, and your father, he was a looker. Very handsome, clean-cut; all the girls talked about him. So I knew she was wrong, but she pressed on, 'Nah, I'm telling you, Bernadette, wait and see. When he drives by to-morrow, we're gonna call him over and you'll see.' Well, we didn't have to wait for that to happen, because later that evening when I came home from the store, my cousin Anthony was sitting on the porch with Papa and guess who was with him?"

"Daddy!" I yelled out.

"None other. He'd been asking around about me. One of his friends knew Anthony and asked him to introduce Randall to me. We were together ever since that day. He would come over to visit, and my father—your grandfather—would sit across from us and pretend he was watching television—when we both knew he was listening to us. I loved your father that first day and still do."

No one said a word. I think we were all consumed with thoughts of daddy and missing him.

* * *

Pulling myself from the thoughts of the past, I picked up the phone to call Keke. The phone kept ringing; just as the answering machine came on, I heard her voice, breathless. "Hello?"

"Hey, girl, what's up?"

"Layla?"

"Oh, you forgot my voice that quick?"

She laughed. "Of course not—hold on a second. I just walked in the door. Let me put my bags down, then we can talk."

"Okay." I missed her even more now that I'd heard her voice.

A short while later, she returned. "What's up, girl? I miss your butt."

"I miss you too."

"How's everything? Are you working or just chillin'? How's Kavan treating you?"

"Like a queen, girl. He's taking care of me like I'm his child—sometimes I have to remind his ass that I'm grown."

She laughed and said, "Diva, diva."

We both grew quiet, each waiting to hear what the other had to say. Not able to take it any longer, I broke down and told her, "I'm lonely, girl. I'm glad I left, but . . . well, you know."

"Yeah, I do."

Without my even having to tell her, I knew she could feel my vibe. She knew I was questioning my actions, my picking up and leaving without giving Jaye one more chance, that a part of me wanted to come home, that I was scared, that I wondered if I was being selfish or if what I was doing was the right thing to do for me.

"Sweetie," she said, "don't stress. You did what you had to do for your peace of mind. You're doing what so many others are afraid to do, and that's going for it; for the gold at the end of the rainbow. We miss you too. You know that, don't you?"

"Yeah, I do."

"Well, all right then. We miss you; you miss us—that's established. What is your next step? What have you done to put yourself closer to that goal of yours?"

See, I knew there was a reason I called Keke. Sometimes I needed that little push, those words of encouragement; to not only feel better about what I was doing, but to know I wasn't crazy as hell for doing it.

By the time we got off the phone, I was psyched, ready to conquer the world, ready to succeed, ready to live life on my terms. I was feeling so good, that when Kavan came busting in the room with a movie, I didn't mind.

"Girl, let's watch *Training Day* with Denzel." He jumped on the bed.

I laughed. If Kavan loved anyone, it was Denzel. I didn't see it. I mean, brother is handsome and all, but the way people act you would think he was the finest thing since slice bread.

"Where's TC?"

"He left; he had to go to the studio."

"You got popcorn? You know we can't watch a movie without popcorn."

"Got it downstairs—popcorn and lemon heads."

I fell out laughing. Kavan was going old-school on a sister. He went downstairs to get the treats, while I popped the disc in.

He came back into the room, and we lay across my bed, neither saying a word until the movie was over.

"Oh my God," I said, "that movie was the shit. Denzel is the man." He had that raw, rugged, thugged-out look in the movie. On him, it was appealing. "I see why he won the Oscar."

Kavan looked at me and laughed. "You've finally come

around. Better late than never, dearie. Hell, he should have won it a long time ago."

He climbed off the bed and kissed me on the cheek. "I'm going to bed now and have wet—oops—I mean sweet dreams."

That night as I lay in bed, I recalled the night of the Oscars. Normally, I didn't watch it, but that night I did because Halle, Denzel, and Will were up for the award, and I knew that one of *our* people would win.

When Halle gave her speech, I felt like I won it along with her; I cried like a baby. People were saying it was the politically correct thing to do—let Black folks win for a change. I didn't care what the reasoning was behind it, all I know is I felt good that night. Good and proud of my people. Like family.

> *Being a winner*
> *To yourself is all that matters*
> *Not what others think*
> *Not what others feel*
> *What's behind what you do*
> *Is it for outsiders*
> *Or for you*

FIRST-TIME LOVE AFFAIR

The gym was crowded even though it was only 6:30 in the morning. I didn't have to teach today, I just came in to get my workout on. That morning I got on the scale and saw that I'd gained five pounds. I couldn't have that. I wanted to at least maintain. Today would be my running day. I looked in the direction of the treadmills and not one was available. *What the hell, was everybody trying to lose weight?*

Pissed, I decided to do the bike instead. As I turned around, I heard someone call out, "Hey, Ms. *Instructor.*"

In my face stood Wesley, looking as buff as he did the first time we met.

"What's up? Not teaching today?"

"No." I figured my curtness would make him keep moving. *Not.*

"Well, you're an early bird."

"As are you."

There was an awkward silence.

"Well, have a nice workout." I glanced towards the treadmills and started moving in that direction when I saw one was available.

He was following me. "Can we go out sometimes?"

"I don't think so."

"Why not? I could show you around. I promise you'll have a good time, and I'll treat you like a lady. We can do dinner, the movies, a show, you name it."

"Like I said—I don't think so."

"Please . . ."

I just looked at him.

"You're going to make a brother beg, aren't you?"

"No—I just want to workout and be left alone." Okay, I knew I was being nasty and I did feel a little bad, but I just wasn't ready to date.

"Okay, how about this—"

I got on the treadmill and adjusted the speed.

"How about I give you my number and you call me tonight. We can talk a little, kick it, and then you'll see I'm a decent man. And maybe, just maybe, I'll convince you to go out with me."

Wanting him to go away, I gave in and said, "Okay."

Looking pleased with himself, he told me, "I'll be right back with the number."

Across the room Quassmirah was watching the whole interaction. She looked a little upset—here she's been coming to this gym for months now, and Wesley never went out his way to talk to her.

I was on the treadmill, when Wesley placed his number on the ledge next to the television. He pressed one more time. "Call me."

"I will," I said, relieved he was leaving me alone.

Before you knew it I was on mile three.

The person on the treadmill next to me finally got off, and boy was I glad. I understand that when you workout, you get funky, but damn, this guy was sweating up a storm, breathing all hard and shit. I could finally stop holding my breath and suffer, through my own making, for the next three miles.

Just as I was getting into my space, I heard someone next to me clearing their throat as though they were trying to get my attention. I looked over.

"What's up, girl?" Quassmirah asked like we were the best of friends and saw each other every day.

"Trying to get my workout on." I hoped she got the hint— I didn't feel like talking.

"Don't you hate when people start talking to you when you're trying to workout, it's like you just want to say, 'Will you shut up.' "

I tried giving her the "take-your-own-advice" look.

She started laughing. "I'm just playing with you. Enjoy your workout. Maybe I'll see you before you leave." She got off the treadmill and walked away.

I have to admit that Quassmirah did appear to be cool as hell. Maybe I needed to put my guard down and befriend someone. Right now the only person in my life was Kavan. *When I'm done, I'll ask her out to lunch.*

QUASSMIRAH

I saw her coming in the mirror. *I wonder what she wants; she didn't have time for me a while ago.* I smiled. "What's up?"

Shifting from side to side, Layla rushed out, "Um, want to have lunch—that is, if you have nothing else to do."

"I'd love to. What time are we talking?"

"How about one? We can meet at the little café down the street."

"Bet."

On that note, Layla walked away.

Well, that was surprising, I thought.

When I arrived home there was a note on the kitchen table from Kavan stating that he would be out of town for a couple of days. He was doing a show at the last minute and would call me later that night.

Sitting on the edge of the bed, I took off my workout gear then decided to take a shower first, and then relax for a couple of hours.

While in the shower the phone rang. I jumped out and went to answer it. "Hello?" I was standing there butt naked, water dripping off my body. *The least I could have done was put on a robe.*

"What's up, girl?" Justice asked.

"Nothing—hold on a second." I went and got a towel, wrapped it around my body. I sat on the bed and picked the phone back up. "You miss me?"

"You know I do—that's why I'm calling."

"I miss you too."

"So, how's L.A. treating you? Are the women fine out there or what?"

I just laughed. His mind was always in one place and on one thing.

"I'm thinking about coming to visit."

I perked up. "I'd like that. When?"

"Maybe sometime next month . . . me and Ali."

"Cool."

Justice cleared his throat and blurted out, "I just thought I'd let you know that I saw Jaye out with a woman."

Why did he have to tell me that? My heart fell to the floor. "So? We're not together anymore—why should I care?"

"Okay, if you say so."

After a moment of silence, I asked, "What did she look like? Who was she?"

"I thought you didn't care."

"I don't, but since you thought enough to tell me, I want to know more."

"Uh huh. I think the girl's name is Lynn. I've seen her around before."

"Damn." I knew just who he was talking about—that slut from the gym. Now that I was gone, she probably came on to Jaye full steam ahead. Wanting to change the subject, I asked him, "Who is your latest hoochie?"

"Now, you know I don't date hoochies."

"Yeah . . . whatever."

"I've decided to go solo for a little while; these women are wearing me down before my time."

I just laughed, knowing his break from women would last no longer than a week.

"You think I'm kidding, don't you?"

"If you say so, I believe you. I just wish I was home to see this solo thing."

We chatted some more and hung up with "I love you's."

I felt an emptiness in my heart and found myself crying over the fact that Jaye went out with someone so soon. I think my pride was hurt. It's like his ass couldn't wait. Glancing over, I reached for my gym bag and thought, *Two can play that game.* I searched inside for Wesley's phone number. Now I knew two wrongs didn't make a right, but it'll damn sure make me feel better. Taking a deep breath, I dialed the number on the card.

The voice on the other end said, "Wesley Jones' office. How may I help you?"

"May I speak with Mr. Jones?"

"He's in a meeting right now. May I ask who's calling?"

"Layla Simone." I could hear the phones ringing in the background.

"Can you hold a second, please?"

Chickening out and not wanting to leave a message, I tried to yell, "That's okay," but she was already gone. I wanted to hang up, but that would've been rude, since I already gave her my name.

A man's voice came on the phone. "Hello?"

"Um, hi, I was waiting to leave a message."

"Layla Simone?"

"Yes."

"This is Wesley. I'm surprised you called."

His voice was like silk. It caught me off guard. "I told you I would."

"I thought you just said that so I would get out of your face, or that it would be a while before you called. This is a nice surprise. I thought maybe you were playing hard to get or something."

"Well, I'm not exactly easy."

"Oh, I wasn't saying that."

"I was only kidding." I found myself laughing, enjoying the flow of the conversation.

"So, I see I have to be on my toes with you."

"A little. The person on the phone said you were busy."

"Nah, I'm just screening my calls."

"Oh." I put the phone in the crock of my neck and grabbed the Neutrogena Almond body oil off the dresser and rubbed it on my body. "So what's your schedule looking like this evening?"

"Why? Are you going to take me up on my offer to dinner?"

"I was thinking about it."

"Is this the same Layla Simone that was in the gym this morning? The one that gave me the cold shoulder?"

Okay, he had me there. I did give him the cold shoulder and might have kept giving it to him if my brother didn't tell me about Jaye and Lynn. "Yes, it is. Are you going to hold it against me? After all, you are a stranger and I was raised not to talk to strangers. I'm new in this area. I can't just accept dates from any and everybody."

"Mind if I ask you what changed your mind?"

Now that was a question I wasn't going to answer honestly. "I just figured why not, we'll be in a public place, what harm can be done?"

Wesley laughed. "All right. How's eight o'clock? I'll send a car for you."

I was quite impressed. "You'll send a car for me?"

"Yes. What's your address?"

I gave it to him.

"That's sounds familiar."

"I'm staying with a friend."

"What's her name?"

"It's a he," I told him, imagining his mind going to work.

"Oh."

"He doesn't mind. He does his thing; I do mine."

"Oh."

"You might have heard of him."

"Oh?"

Teasing him, I asked, "Is that all you can say, 'Oh'?"

"I don't know what else to say until you tell me who this mysterious person is."

"Kavan Jones."

"Oh, I see." He laughed like he understood. "How do you know him?"

Although Wesley's forte was music and Kavan's was comedy, it was still entertainment. If you were high up on the who's who list, you knew that Kavan was gay. It wasn't something he hid any more.

"Childhood friends."

"Oh. So . . . is eight o'clock good for you?"

"Yes, it is."

"Good. I can't wait to see you."

"Okay. Bye." The fact that he said he couldn't wait to see me wasn't lost on me.

I definitely had a busy day ahead of me—lunch with Quassmirah and then dinner with Wesley. Glancing at the clock, I saw there was no way I'd be taking the nap I'd planned. Between my conversation with my brother and talking to Wesley, the time had flown by.

Walking inside the café, I saw that Quassmirah was already there. She looked up from a book she was reading and waved me over.

The café was very quaint, obviously for artists. The walls were filled with paintings. As I walked by them, I glanced at the names, not recognizing any. *I must ask the waitress about it later.* The paintings were erotic; something I was sure Kavan would be interested in. There was one on the wall with two men embracing, just their silhouettes and the flickers of candles surrounding them. I knew he would love it. Depending on the price, I was thinking of purchasing it for him.

The tables against the walls had computers on them and were filled with people, with the drink of their choice, typing away. There was also a back room with a little stage on it.

Quassmirah stood up and hugged me. She was wearing black leather capris and a tube top.

"I like this place," I told her while sitting; "it can definitely get your creative juices flowing."

"Are you an actress?" Quassmirah asked.

"Nah, my thing is writing. And yours?"

She laughed because she knew and I knew that to be in California, you had to have something going on. Something artistic.

"I'm an actress and a singer. Actually, I sing with a band. We're performing tonight. Would you like to come?"

"Nah, I have a date."

"Really? So soon? May I ask with whom?"

Might as well tell her, she wanted me to hook up with him so bad. "Wesley."

"Get out of here," Quassmirah said. "Where are you going?"

"I'm not sure, but he's sending a car for me."

"That's nice." Quassmirah sounded sincere. "Well, maybe you and him can stop by the club I'm performing at."

I couldn't believe Quassmirah had a plan just that quick. "I don't know about making suggestions on the first date."

"I understand." *Now to plan two—playing this friendship card right and getting her to pass Wesley my demo.* "So, tell me, how do you like it here so far?"

Before I could answer, the waitress came over to take our order. Knowing I would be going out to dinner later, I ordered a light appetizer and some seltzer water.

"It's okay. It's just an adjustment being away from family and all," I told her when the waitress walked away.

"I can understand. I know what it was like when I first came out here."

By the time our salads arrived, we were discussing men. How the conversation went that way, I had no idea. Quassmirah had the skill for getting people to open up.

"Girl, my last boyfriend was an asshole, but his skills in bed made me overlook it. I was out there, strung out, calling him constantly, sweating his ass. Come to find out, I wasn't the only one; he had other women."

"How did you find out?"

Quassmirah frowned. "The worst way possible. It was like a movie. I tried surprising him at his office with lunch. When I walked in, his secretary wasn't at her desk, so I walked into his office. Lo and behold, his secretary was on her knees sucking his dick!"

"Get the hell out of here! What did he do?"

"He just looked at me, smiled and said, 'Do you want to join us?' "

"You're lying."

"If I'm lying, I'm flying. But you know what, I did that to myself; I set myself up."

"Why do you feel that way? No one deserves to be treated like shit."

"You're right, but I put myself out there. He felt he could do anything and say anything to me. I'd done things with him I hadn't done and won't do with anyone else."

I was all ears. *This shit was getting good.* "Like what?"

"Like a threesome." Quassmirah didn't seem the least bit embarrassed.

"With another woman?" I knew she wasn't talking about with another man, because no manly man, no man who thinks he's all that, would allow it.

"Yeah, girl, I allowed another woman into our bedroom and it seems like all hell broke loose afterwards."

I couldn't help wondering why she was telling me all her

business like it was nothing, because if I did some shit like that, it would go to my grave with me. But who was I to judge?

I knew that the threesome thing was every man's fantasy. Well, at least my brothers' and Jaye's. One night Jaye and I were watching the Spice channel, and there was a threesome going on. Even I had to admit, it looked more than entertaining.

"Would you ever do something like that?" he asked.

"Why? Would you?"

"Maybe." He looked at me out of the corner of his eye.

Me being the tease that I was, I decided to go for broke. "Well . . . it depends."

"On what?"

"On the circumstances. On the person. On a lot of things."

"Like?"

"I would have to choose the person, get to know them first. And we'd have to be friends."

"Why do y'all have to become friends, especially if it's all about the sex?"

I knew he was going to say that because, one time, my brothers were talking, and of course Justice was going through some drama with this chick he was seeing. They decided to do the threesome thing, and she befriended the girl.

After they went through with the act, it became too much for him to handle. The girl he was seeing was hanging with the other chick too much. They were always on the phone, always going out. He said he started to feel like she was his competition, and he wasn't too keen on that idea. Eventually the women became a couple.

"Why not? Why shouldn't we be friends? My stuff is too precious to be sharing with just anyone."

"Because it's like it becomes a 'you-and-her' thing and not an 'our' thing. The woman's purpose is to come and go."

I laughed. "I don't think so."

We let the subject drop, only for it to come up occasionally, although I knew the shit wasn't going to happen. Not in this lifetime.

"Girl, your ass was brave," I told Quassmirah.

"No, I was stupid." She shook her head. "Enough about me and my past—did you have a man in Jersey?"

"Yeah. We were together since high school."

"What happened?"

"My coming here broke us up."

"Damn."

I waited on her to ask the question everyone tended to ask: "Why didn't y'all get married?"

"Do you think you and him will ever get back together?"

"It's not something I think about," I lied, replying in a tone that suggested I didn't want to discuss it anymore.

Lunch ended up being a treat. We had a nice time talking and laughing. I think I'd made a new friend. Or not to be so hasty with words, I think I'd made a new associate, because like Kavan said, "Don't just give your friendship away; let a person prove they are worthy of it, because a bitch will walk all over you in a heartbeat if you allow them to."

New faces
New places
New beginnings
New endings
Twists and turns
Ups and downs
Not knowing
What's around
New faces and new places

TREATED LIKE ROYALTY

That evening as I got ready for my date, I thought about Jaye and how I was a fool for waiting so long. Here I almost let life just pass me by. Thank God I saw the light.

I wanted to look exceptionally good for our first date. I was sure he was used to gorgeous women hounding him, especially being in the music business with access to video ho's and wannabe singers. I just imagined how many women approached him on a daily basis.

I decided to wear a red silk shirtdress—my favorite color and the color Jaye didn't like for me to wear when going out, because he said, "It's like a woman is calling for attention." It had a V-neck that exposed just the right amount of cleavage and stopped mid-thigh. I put on the dress with no stockings and strapped, high-heeled sandals. I wore my hair pulled back into a ponytail, nice and tight, to show my cheekbones, with little makeup and small, diamond hoop earrings.

Looking in the mirror, I liked what stood before me and smiled. *A sister looked good.* Before I knew it, the doorbell rang. "Coming!" When I opened the door, I was shocked to see a limo parked outside my house. I knew he said he was sending a car, but damn, he *really* sent a car.

"Hello. I'm here to pick up Layla Simone," the driver—a white man, at that—said.

"I'm her." I was all teeth. "I'll be out in a minute."

The driver walked away, and I went to take one last look in the mirror. After making sure the house was locked up, I walked out to the car. The driver held the door for me, and I climbed in the back.

Flowers in hand, Wesley looked debonair.

"This is nice," I told him while getting in the car; "I feel special."

"A beautiful woman needs to be treated special."

I was feeling it, let me tell you. "Throw on the charm, throw on the charm," I told him, and together we laughed.

Wesley handed me the flowers and looked me up and down.

I could see the approval in his eyes. I returned the favor and made sure he could see the approval in mine as well.

Wesley was wearing some serious cream linen pants that fit loosely, with a soft-yellow shirt tucked in at the waist. He had on a brown Gucci belt and Gucci sandals. He was "bling blinging."

Taking the flowers out of his hands and sniffing them, I looked up and asked, "So where are we going?"

"To dinner, and then if you feel up to it, maybe to hear this band someone told me about."

We both leaned back and relaxed into the seat, while the driver rolled up the partition that separated us from him.

"What kind of music do you like?" he asked.

"I like it all—jazz, hip-hop, R&B. I'm not prejudiced when it comes to music, as long as it sounds good. I have to admit, I'm partial to Phyllis Hyman."

He smiled. "A girl after my own heart." Wesley tapped on the partition and told the driver to put on Ms. Hyman. Which surprised me.

"Betcha by Golly Wow!" started playing, and Wesley moved closer to me, resting his arms behind me. "I'm glad you said yes to dinner. Like I told you on the phone, I was quite surprised. I thought I was going to have to pull out all the stops to get you to say yes."

"Well, here I am, and it looks like you did that anyway. I figured, why sit in the house by myself when you were so smooth in your approach?" Of course, there was no way I was going to tell him that my heart was broken and I needed comfort; that he was my band-aid for the night.

We sat in silence listening to the music, until the car stopped.

"We're here."

I looked out the window to see where we were. La' Ames was the name of the restaurant. It was the perfect night for such a place. The driver let us out the car, and together we walked in the restaurant.

"Ah, Mr. Jones," the maitre d' said, "you're here. Follow me."

"You must come here often."

"It's one of my favorite places, and I wanted to share it with you."

I could see why, on ambiance alone. The restaurant had a serene and romantic vibe to it. There were exotic plants everywhere, soft lighting with tinges of red and yellow. The music playing over the intercom was low; it was Sade. We were led to an intimate table in the corner, where there was a bottle of champagne and two flute glasses.

Wesley pulled my seat out for me to sit down. I was so nervous, my heart was racing. I hadn't been on a date in a long time and wanted to say the right things and be amusing, yet charming.

Wesley poured a glass of champagne and handed it to me. "Let's make a toast."

"Okay." I hoped he meant he would be the one making it.

"To us and you taking a chance on me."

We clinked and sipped.

"So, what do you do? What brought you out to California?"

"I'm a writer. I write screenplays, and I'm working on a novel."

"Wow! Have you ever had anything published?"

"Yes, in a few magazines, but I'm ready for the big time."

"I hear that. I know people . . . production people. Maybe I can pass some of your work along."

Now why would he do that when he's never even read my stuff? He's trying to get the booty, big-time. "That would be nice, but don't feel obligated."

"I won't, but if I can help a sister out, why not?"

I thought that was sweet as hell of him, because when I first decided to step out and try to do this thing, I wrote an author/director/producer and asked for his help, his assistance, some sort of advice. What I got back was an "I'm out for self. The letter you wrote me was nice, but since you have already had things published, you should know the steps" response. I thought that was bullshit, because I knew that when I blew up, I'd be bringing people along for the ride.

That thought and memory made me decide to tell him about Quassmirah and her band. "There's this girl I just befriended that goes to the gym. She's a singer—"

"Does she have a demo?"

"She's in the process of making one."

"Well, there's really nothing I can do if she hasn't made one already."

Shifting in my seat, I told him, "She performs in a band and I'd like to hear what she sounds like. Maybe on our next date we could go hear her." (Yep, I was getting ahead of myself.)

"If that means you plan on seeing me again, we can do that."

The waiter came over to take our orders.

"I never received a menu," I told him.

"Oh, that's okay. I know the menu by heart. I'll order for the both of us."

Now that was something I didn't like, a man ordering for me, but I decided to let it go, since this was the first date.

Over dinner, we made small talk while enjoying the delicious meal. We were finishing up when the waiter came over and asked if we wanted any dessert.

Wesley looked at me.

"No thanks."

"You want us to put this on your tab?" the waiter asked Wesley.

I was getting more impressed by the minute.

"Yes." Wesley pulled out his wallet, took out thirty dollars, and gave it to the waiter.

Graciously, the waiter said, "Thanks."

"You're welcome."

I went to stand up, but not before the waiter pulled my chair out and said, "Enjoy your evening, lovely lady."

We were back in the car and I have to tell you, the champagne had me feeling rather tipsy. I moved closer to him and placed myself in the nook of his arm. "So tell me about yourself."

"What do you want to know?"

"How you've become the man you are today? What brought you here from New York? Do you have any brothers or sisters?"

"Oh, so you want to know my life story?"

"If you'll share."

"Well, I'm from Brooklyn, and I'm the oldest of six kids. I'm also the most successful. I always knew I would be in the music business, just didn't know how."

Before he could go on, the driver pulled over.

"We're here," Wesley said.

I looked out the window and saw that we were in front of a club. "That was quick."

"We were only a couple of blocks away. Are you ready to go in?"

Honestly, I was ready to go home and sleep. The champagne went from having me tipsy to straight tired. I was really going against myself that night, letting him order for me, now going in a club, when what I really wanted to do was go home. "Sure, I'm ready."

The driver let us out the car, and once again, we were treated like royalty.

Hand in hand they walked in the club, and for a brief moment all eyes were on them. The men were wondering, *Who is this fine woman with Wesley? And where did he find her?* The women were wondering, *What does she have that I don't?*

Both Layla and Wesley were oblivious to the looks. Layla glanced up at the stage and started laughing when she saw Quassmirah up there. Layla tapped Wesley on the shoulder, and he turned around. "What's so funny?" he asked.

Layla pointed towards the stage. "Talk about coincidences. You see the girl on stage? The lead singer?"

"Damn, she looks familiar."

"That's the girl I was telling you about, the singer that works out at the same gym."

Wesley took another look and frowned. "Does this mean I won't get a second date with you?"

Layla smiled. "No, it doesn't. Let's get a drink and then let's go say hello." Layla started walking towards the bar with Wesley traveling behind her.

When they reached the bar, the bartender bypassed everyone and came over to them, slapping Wesley five. "What's up, my brother?" he asked. "Who's the *unlucky* lady today?" He winked at Layla.

"Czar, this is Layla. Layla, this is my boy, Czar."

Czar reached for her hand, and when she gave it to him, instead of shaking it, he kissed it. "The pleasure is all mine. All mine."

Layla blushed. "Czar? That's an odd name for a black man."

He just laughed and asked, "What are you drinking, my queen?"

A night out
Just what I need
Ready to party
Let my hair down
A night on the town
No reasons to hide
New place
New face
A whole scene
Letting go of my inhibitions
If you know what I mean

WESLEY

Layla wasn't only gorgeous, but kind, gentle, and had a sense of humor. Shit, I thought I could make her my wife. I know you're wondering how I could come out my face with something like that and I hardly even knew this girl. Well, let me tell you, just like a woman knows, so does a man. I was going to make her mine, come hell or high water. I met the one, and Layla was it.

I was raised in a house with five women. I was the middle child. My sisters were a trip. They would use a brother up and discard him like he was yesterday's news if he didn't meet their expectations—I'm talking about financially and physically. I would watch them and be like, *No woman is ever going to treat me the way they treated the knuckleheads that walked through our door.* They were worse than some brothers I knew.

"Why do y'all treat men like that?" I'd ask them.

"We have to get them before they get us," was the standard reply.

The funny thing is, I knew what they were talking about because I was a playa myself. Me and my boys, the more pussy we could get, the better. The more women we conquered, the better. We were on missions.

My father walked all over my mother. My sisters saw this

and would always try to tell my mother to leave him, but she didn't.

"When we married I made a vow to God—for better or for worse," she'd always say.

On one hand, I respected her for it, but on the other, I wanted her to leave him too. Eventually, my father stopped all the messing around, and it wasn't by choice, it was by fate. He was injured in a freak accident. Walking under a ladder, it tipped and fell on him, breaking his collar bone. He was now paralyzed and living in a nursing home. I guess, my mother got her revenge.

Born and raised in Brooklyn, I'd seen it all—poverty, murder, riches (mostly from illegal activity) and all kinds of scams. I got caught up in the drug game through my uncles and my older sister's man. I never planned to stay in it long; I just wanted enough money to start my own business.

But you couldn't just quit the game like that. I had to up and leave, move across the country. In my journeys, I'd dealt with different types of women. Gold diggers mostly. So when I met Layla, I knew instantly that she wasn't a gold digger. Especially when I told her who I was and she didn't know.

Yeah, she could have been faking it, but being around sincerity through my mom, I felt like I could read the signs. I was also ready to settle down and have children. Hell, I was getting old and a family would be nice. So, hopefully this Layla and Wesley thing was going to work out.

The love of my life
To be my wife
To share my future
For better or worse
For richer for poorer
A lady in public
In bed
A whore

WHAT DID I DO?

My date with Wesley was one of the best dates I'd had in a long time. Heck, it was one of the first dates I'd had in a long time. It was a damn shame I ended up acting like a first-class whore.

We were still in the club, nursing drink number two. We hadn't made it up to the stage, we were too busy laughing and joking with Czar.

Czar reminded me so much of my brother Justice; he was a ladies' man too. All he talked about was his women, what they did, what he could make them do. Not in a disrespectful manner, but in an amusing manner. He had a familiar spirit, and I enjoyed being around him. Which was obvious, because he had me laughing hysterically.

At one point Wesley looked at me, and I could have sworn I saw a frown. I convinced myself, I was bugging.

"Don't you have some customers to tend to?" he asked Czar, a little irritation in his voice.

Czar heard the tone. "You're right, my man. If you need anything, let me know."

* * *

I came to find out that Czar and Wesley went way back, all the way back to Brooklyn as teenagers. Wesley was the first to leave New York and migrate to L.A. Once Czar came to visit, he got hooked on the money, the women, and the flashy cars. He ended up crashing with Wesley, who was already doing his thing on the music tip for over a year.

In Brooklyn they were both "in the life"—drug dealers, high up, making serious dough. Big wheelies. The drug life was getting too dangerous, too deadly. Turf was no longer being respected, people were no longer being respected, and even the drugs were no longer being respected, meaning they were being tampered with. It came down to wanting to live, so the safest and easiest way to do it was to move across the country.

Czar didn't want to leave Brooklyn. He felt that Wesley was taking the money and running. It wasn't until he got shot in a stand-off, that he decided enough was enough. He called Wesley, who told him to take the next flight out and chill with him until he decided what to do.

Once he visited a second time, he decided to stay. He was actually the owner of the bar. He took the money he saved from the drug life and purchased it. He just worked as a bartender occasionally, because he liked to be around the people.

"So, are you ready to introduce me to your friend?" Wesley asked.

"Sure," I said.

As we approached the stage, Quassmirah started singing another song. She looked beautiful in her ankle-length, form-fitting, flesh-colored gown. The working out she did was obvious from the way her dress fit, and as I looked closer, I noticed her eyes were a different color. She was wearing contacts, light-brown, and justice they did.

Her voice left a little to be desired. Not that she sounded

bad, but with people like Mary J. Blige, Whitney Houston, and Mariah Carey out there, you had to be careful when you say you can sing. She didn't have a strong voice, although it was clear and pretty.

I looked over at Wesley to see if he was feeling her. I couldn't tell.

"How do you like her?"

"She definitely has a look. Very sexy. Her band is tight; she has a presence."

"What about her voice?"

Wesley looked at me. "Well, what do you think?"

"I think she has a pretty voice. It might not be as strong as some of those out there, but isn't that something she could work on? Half the singers out there can barely sing as it is."

Before he could answer, Quassmirah was upon us.

QUASSMIRAH

I saw them the minute they walked through the door. I saw everyone the minute they walked through the door. Hell, you never know who with power may step in. Home girl came through. I didn't think she would. It took them long enough to leave the bar and listen to me. As soon as I had their full attention, I was ready to put it down and I did. That was my best performance yet.

When an opportunity knocks
Be prepared
Be fearless
Be strong
Take advantage
Act as if you belong

BACK TO THE DATE

Quassmirah hugged me like we were long-lost relatives or something, and whispered in my ear, "I knew you'd look out for a sister."

I didn't have the heart to tell her that it was coincidental.

Not waiting for an introduction, she introduced herself to Wesley.

"I see you at the gym," he told her. "How come you never told me you were a singer?"

"I was just waiting for the opportunity; I'm sure you get hounded as it is now."

"You're right about that." He pulled a card out of his jacket pocket and told her to give him a call.

"I most definitely will."

We left shortly afterwards, with Quassmirah promising to call us both. How I let him talk me into going to his house, I didn't know. Maybe it was the liquor. Maybe it was the promise of a late-night swim in his pool or chilling in the Jacuzzi by candlelight. Whatever it was, I found myself standing on the deck.

Wesley stepped up behind me and put his hands around my waist. "Do you want to get in the Jacuzzi?"

Stepping away, I asked, "How? I don't have a bathing suit."

"I have bathing suits here."

I must have given him a look that said, "You're out of your mind if you think I'm going to wear someone else's bathing suit."

"I have brand new ones. I keep them here for my nieces when they come to visit, or for videos."

There was no way I could tell if he was lying or not, and I *did* want to get in the Jacuzzi, so I said, "Yes."

He pointed to a door and said, "That's the changing room. There's a drawer in there with the suits in them. I'm sure one will fit you."

I didn't see Wesley and figured he went inside to change, so I entered the Jacuzzi first, leaned back, and closed my eyes, finding myself getting lost in the heat and the romance of the night.

"Hey, beautiful." Wesley interrupted my peace by climbing in beside me.

I opened my eyes and was amazed at his body once again. *Being here is not a good idea.* I should have left that instant.

From the side of the Jacuzzi, he produced some strawberries and whipped cream.

"And what, may I ask, are you going to do with that?"

"Relax and let me show you."

I let him feed them to me. Yes, I was caught up in the moment.

It took us all of ten minutes to start kissing, and two more for me to be straddled on his lap, tongue down his throat. It felt like I hadn't been up that close on a man in ages. I could feel that familiar tingle between my legs and found myself pressing up against the bulge in his swimming briefs.

He placed his hands on either side of my face and pulled my lips away from his. He looked me in the eye. "Do you want to stay the night?"

That question brought me back to reality. I didn't even know this man, and here I was, all up in his lap, grinding like a teenager, in a bathing suit nonetheless. Climbing off his lap and sitting next to him, I said, "I'm embarrassed. I think I want to go home."

"Embarrassed?"

"Yes. For acting like a hoochie. Like a groupie."

"Damn, girl, we're grown, consenting adults. I know you're not. You didn't come after me; I came after you."

"That doesn't make my behavior any better."

He stepped out the Jacuzzi and reached over for my hand. I gave it to him. He passed me a towel. I wrapped myself up in it and followed him into the house.

"I don't want you to leave."

"What we want and what I should do are two different things."

"Please stay. We can just chill and watch a movie. I won't try anything, I promise."

I was still unsure.

"I have a black film collection. You can pick something out, and we'll watch it together. Come on, let's take a look."

I gave in and followed him. He wasn't lying when he said a collection. He had films dating as far back as the 1920s. I chose *Lady Sings the Blues* with Diana Ross and Billy Dee Williams.

"I'm going to go and put my clothes back on," I told him.

When I returned to the sitting room he was already dressed and on the couch. We watched the movie while sipping on wine. Once again we ended up kissing.

For me, one of the most important things in being intimate with a man was whether or not he could kiss. I couldn't stand a man that covered my whole face with his mouth or left wet spots. A sloppy kisser, I can do without. I liked to be teased with the lips—light pecks, a little tongue. No ear action—can't stand that. I liked to have the back of my neck massaged lightly.

Wesley did all these things. I was pleasantly surprised. It

came to a head when I felt his hands moving towards my breast. I reached up and pulled his hands down. "I don't want to have sex." I figured I'd just come out and say it. "Maybe I've let things go too far with the kissing and all. Maybe I . . ."

Standing up, Wesley said, "Relax, baby doll; you don't have to do anything you don't want to do. I would like for you to stay the night with me—no sex; I just want to lay next to you."

Yeah, right. "I'd rather go home; I think it's best. I don't want to rush into anything. How about we talk tomorrow?"

He agreed with a little hesitation.

I found myself riding home in the limo dozing, his arms around me. When I arrived home, I went straight to my room and collapsed across the bed. I was exhausted physically and mentally. I dozed off thinking about Wesley.

Pleasure
Was within my reach
But I let it go
Afraid
To turn on
What's been off
For so long

FEELS LIKE THE FIRST
DAY OF SCHOOL

I was sitting in class touching up a script when in walked the "blackest" white man I'd ever seen. His walk, his talk, and his style of dressing were obviously influenced by my people. I just knew this could not be my teacher.

"What's up, class? My name is Jonathan. I'm one of the instructors for this workshop. Every week for the next eight weeks I'll be rotating with a couple of other instructors. That way you will not get bored, and you will also learn about the different aspects of the entertainment business."

I had no idea who this man was, but it was obvious he was someone with status. I glanced around the room and noticed the other students were sitting on the edge of their seats. The first day of the workshop was quick and smooth. We didn't do much writing; it was more of a "get-to-know-one-another" day. We talked about ourselves and our goals, why we were interested in writing for Hollywood, the pros and cons of the business. We were given an assignment to write a half-hour sitcom and bring it in to be critiqued in two days.

"Two days?" one of the students asked. "Isn't that a bit much?"

"A bit much?" Jonathan chastised. "If you think that, then you don't need to be here."

I was glad someone else asked the question, because I was thinking the same thing.

"You see," Jonathan went on, "this is California, and it's all about working under pressure. If you can't do it, the next person will. People are a-dime-a-dozen in this industry. Talent is everywhere. You have to be in it to win it. It's a dog-eat-dog world."

He was putting it down, and no one said a word; we just listened.

"So hopefully, you'll be back tomorrow and ready to go, because by the time I'm done with you this week, you will have perfected writing a sitcom. This is an intense class; be prepared for a challenge and to work your asses off."

I'll tell you what—Mr. Jonathan made me anxious to get this thing called success off the ground. I couldn't wait to get home and start on my script. After class, some of the students went to have lunch together. They invited me, but I declined. Me and Kavan were going shopping.

When I arrived home, Kavan told me there was a message from Wesley on the phone. "Two messages, girl—what did you do to him?"

"Worked my magic."

"I know you ain't sleep with him, Ms. Thang."

"I ain't that easy."

"Good. And don't be. Remember he's rich, handsome, and hundreds of women want him and may have had him—don't let his ass use you."

Now that was information he didn't have to tell me, I was not about to get used. I'm not stupid nor naïve. Yes, I'd only had one boyfriend, but I'd seen it happen—women using my brothers, and my brothers using women.

I swear that's what turned Justice into a playa. He was in love with this one girl, Kenya. I mean really in love to the point that he was thinking about marrying her. They met at my bookstore. He came to pick me up and was waiting at the counter. (My car was in the shop and Jaye was working.)

"Can't you hurry it up?" he asked, rushing me to close up.

This made me move even slower. I loved agitating him. "Why are you in a hurry?"

He looked at his watch and said, "It's a Saturday evening—what do you think?"

I took that to mean he had a date. Barely a weekend went by that he didn't.

"Can't you get someone else to close for—" He stopped mid-sentence and stared in the direction of the magazine rack.

I looked up to see what held his attention. When I saw her I knew. She was attractive. She wore very little makeup, hair cornrowed up into a ponytail. She was wearing jeans that looked poured on, black boots, and a sheer white shirt with a black bra underneath. She moved as if she owned the space and had not a care in the world.

Natural, yet beautiful, was how he described her to our mother, when he told her he'd met the one.

"Who is that?" He asked as if I knew every customer that walked in the store.

This time he was lucky. "I don't know her name, but she attends Tuesday's reading group."

"Introduce me to her."

"Didn't I just tell you I don't know her name? Shit, you ain't shy—go introduce yourself."

He took another look at his watch and said, "Nah, you know once I put it down, it's on." He looked over in her direction. "But you best believe I will be here Tuesday."

I just looked at him and laughed. "Yeah, right."

Do you know he actually showed up. She gave him a hard way to go too. She told him they could only be friends and that she wasn't looking for a relationship because she'd just gotten out of one. Not used to being turned down, this made him pursue her aggressively. He started spending all his free time with her, buying her things, taking her places. This went on for quite some time. Eventually, he brought her over to meet the family.

I tried to click with her, but there was something that didn't sit right. I watched her like a hawk. My brother was spending money like water, and she was still saying she wasn't ready to be in a relationship. I felt as if she was using him. I didn't want to interfere because he was a grown man. And what if I was wrong?

Well, I wasn't. One evening, the same day Justice told me he was falling in love with her and was thinking about proposing, me and Ali were out to dinner. Lo and behold, I glanced around the room, and there she sat in the restaurant with some guy, holding hands across the table.

"What do you think we should do?" Ali asked me when I brought it to his attention.

"I think we should go over there so she knows we see her ass."

"Well, do your thing, girl."

Not one to let my brothers get played, I went over to the table, cleared my throat.

She looked up and shock was on her face. She moved her hand from under the guy's.

"Well, hello there," I said.

"Hi."

"Aren't you going to introduce me to your date?" I put emphasis on the word date to let her know I wasn't blind.

"Um, um—"

"You know what—never mind. Instead, how about we talk later?" I walked away.

Me, I would have done everything in my power to leave, but I guess she figured she was already busted.

I wanted to smack her, but I did one better. I went back to my table, pulled out my cell phone, and called Justice to tell him he needed to get down to the restaurant as soon as possible.

"Why?"

"Your woman is here with someone and it looks intimate."

"They could just be friends. She has male friends, just like I have female friends."

"Listen, you could be right, but I have a feeling in this case you're not. Ali is here with me, and he can vouch for it. I passed Ali the phone.

"Yeah, man, it looks like more than friendship to me."

They met on the way out. Justice didn't cause a scene. He watched her for a while and, when he'd seen enough, went up to her and said, "I'd like my key."

My mouth dropped open. I didn't know she had a key to his place. That was something he'd never done before—give a female access to his kingdom.

A few words were exchanged, and my brother was left heartbroken. Of course, she tried calling him up and getting back in his good graces, but he wasn't hearing it.

So as I was saying . . . I knew about users and the used. I reassured Kavan it wouldn't happen here. Oh no, not to Layla Simone.

Not one to be played
So step back
Don't want to put you in your place
Not one to be played
Not in this lifetime
Violating my space

MY! HOW TIME FLIES

The workshop was going well. It was worth every penny I'd paid. I felt that my writing was improving and that it was time to start the submission process to production companies. After class I joined some of the students for drinks and arrived home intoxicated.

There was a message on the kitchen table from Kavan to call Keke. I sat my books down, made myself a cup of tea, relaxed on the couch, and called her. "What's up, girl?" I said, stretching out. I was dead tired, because not only did I have the workshop, but I had to teach two classes at the gym as well. Physical and brain power were all used up.

"Nothing. Just missing your ass and due a vacation. I was thinking about coming to see you."

I perked up immediately. "Get out!"

"Yep. What do you think?"

"What do you mean, what do I think? I think, yes, get on the next flight, hurry it up."

She laughed. "It's nice to know I'm missed too."

"That you are."

After a few minutes of conversation, it was obvious something was up, that this wasn't just a social call. When I asked her what was going on, she told me she was thinking of becoming partners with someone.

"My only concern is I've been on my own for so long, I don't know if I could deal with another staff and too many personalities up in here. Plus, it'll root me here forever."

"What? Do you plan on moving? Why would you be concerned about something like that?"

"I don't know. It just seems like I've always played it safe, always stayed close to home. Sometimes I think about just 'up and leaving' like you did."

Hearing Keke say this threw me for a loop, because she never talked about stepping out. "Well, whatever you decide to do, just know that I've got your back." I was itching to ask about Jaye, but decided to leave it alone. *What I don't know won't hurt me.*

She would be arriving in a week. That week couldn't go by fast enough.

As soon as we hung up, the phone rang again. I picked up on the second ring and wished I hadn't—it was Wesley.

Homeboy was sweating a sister; calling me every day. Now don't get me wrong, all the attention was flattering, considering there were tons of women out there he could choose from. My question was, *Why me? What made me stand out from the rest of them?*

I couldn't handle this shit—being heartbroken, living in a new city and missing my old, and seeing a new man. I already felt like I was falling apart at the seams. So the added pressure of Wesley was a bit much.

I'll tell you what'd been going on and let you decide if I was blowing it out of proportion. Maybe I was. I even discussed it with Keke, who told me I needed to just go with the flow.

Well, you know about the first date we went on . . . when I acted like a hoochie, went to his house, and allowed myself to get felt up. Well, that was nothing compared to the second date.

Wesley was charming, amusing, handsome, and rich, and had this way about him that made you feel like a lady. So I said, "Yes," when he asked about taking me out again.

The date was romantic. It was like a scene out of a movie. He had me so impressed. I ended up having sex with him. Maybe it was the California air or the fact that I was lonely. It wasn't too much of a waste of time. One complaint, and a major one at that—homeboy did not eat the coochie. What a disappointment! Therefore, I did not go down on him. I probably wouldn't have anyway. These lips had only been around one man's ding-a-ling, and we all know whose.

We'd made a date for lunch, but I didn't know that he had a picnic planned. He picked me up from home, this time in his vehicle: a white Mercedes coupe. When we pulled up to the park, he got out and went to the trunk of his car.

"What are you doing? I thought you said we were going to lunch?"

"We are. Come and see."

I walked to where he stood and was pleasantly surprised to see a checkered red-and-white picnic basket and wine. The fact that his secretary probably picked everything up didn't lessen the impact. I thought it was romantic, considerate, and thoughtful.

"This is nice." I kissed him on the cheek.

He pulled the basket and a blanket out of the car, and I grabbed the wine. We found a spot under a tree. In the basket was pasta salad, fruit salad, cheese and crackers.

We had such a nice time that when he invited me over to swim, I said, "Yes." When we got to his place, I used the same swimsuit I'd used before. I guess you could say I claimed it. *This time I would be taking it home.* He swam circles around me, but I didn't care, I was having a ball. It was when I pulled a muscle that all hell broke loose.

"Owww!" I yelled, holding on to my leg.

He swam over to me. "What's wrong? What happened?"

"I don't know. I think I pulled something."

"Come on, let's get out the pool and let me massage it."

Not one to turn down a massage, I said, "Okay."

We got out the pool and I lay on my stomach across the lounge.

"I'll be right back." He walked off and returned quickly with some oil. "Where does it hurt?"

I touched my quads and closed my eyes.

He poured a cinnamon-scented oil down the length of both my legs and rubbed it in gently, rubbing and kneading the sore one first.

I opened my legs a little wider, to get the full effect.

He went from one leg to the other. "How does that feel?"

I moaned; it felt too good for words.

He moved slowly down to my feet, playing with my toes. His hands moved up the sides of my legs slowly, touching my bikini bottom. Then he stopped.

I surprised myself by saying, "Go on," and he did, gently massaging my backside.

Okay, now that was where I messed up. I loved having my ass rubbed, especially when making love. I felt like it opened me up more. Too scared to say anything, I kept shifting my body. I felt the juices moistening my walls.

Wesley went to the small of my back and ran his manicured nails down my spine, causing me to arch, and tapped his fingers up and down.

I tried to turnover.

"Wait," he said.

I could hear the desire in his voice.

He bent over and ran his tongue down the length of my back. He stopped at my panties and pulled them down.

It was at this point that I should have stopped him, but I was feeling it. I didn't and couldn't say a word.

"Now turn over."

I did and looked him in the eyes. Slowly I roamed the length of his body and eyed his penis, which was thick, long, and covered with a condom. When and how he got undressed and put that on, I had no idea because I thought his hands were on me the whole time.

My hormones were screaming, and every inch of me was ready to shut them up. So there I was, on my back, waiting to be caressed, kissed, and possibly licked.

None of the above happened. He grabbed my hips, pulled me to the edge of the table, and entered me with one quick thrust. He stayed in the one spot and just rotated his hips around and around.

I grabbed his hips and tried to get him to thrust, but he wasn't having it. He was going to do it his way, and I was glad he did. He had his eyes closed.

"Look at me," I said. I wanted to see how good it felt to him.

He asked me to wrap my legs around his waist. I did and he plunged deeper.

A short while later, he arched his back and pressed inside me as far as he could go and let out a moan. "Damn, girl." He withdrew and wrapped the towel around him. "I'll be right back. Stay right there."

When he returned, he had a washcloth with him, and the condom was gone. He wiped me clean.

Still didn't taste it.

I told him I wanted to shower, and we ended up taking one together. Of course, he wanted to get busy again, but I wasn't having it. I was entirely too sore, embarrassed, and ready to go home and finish myself off.

So now a brother was sweating a sister, calling me and coming up to me in the gym. It wasn't that I didn't want to be bothered; it's just that, I needed time to process what took place between us. Heck, I needed time to process the lack of foreplay and to decide if I wanted to be intimate with someone whose only concern sexually was to get his nut.

Anyway, when I answered the phone and heard his voice, I decided to be honest with him.

'I've been calling and calling you and you haven't returned any of my calls."

"I know. I've just been so busy between school and teaching, I haven't had the time to get back to you."

"Really?" He sounded as if he didn't believe me.

"Yes, really. Look . . . Wesley . . . maybe we're moving too fast."

"What do you mean, 'moving too fast'? We're just kicking it, being friends."

"I know. It just—it just feels like more. I slept with you and I shouldn't have."

"Is that what this is about? You're ashamed?"

"Partly."

"Please . . . we're grown, we're adults, we did what we wanted to do."

"I know. It's just that I don't normally sleep with people I just met; it's out of character."

"Normally when a woman says something like that, I don't believe her. But with you I do, and I'm telling you don't stress over it. Like I said, no harm in being friends. If you don't want it to, it won't happen again."

All I could say was "Okay."

WESLEY

Okay, she'd been giving me the brush-off and I needed to know why. I wasn't used to this shit. No one could be that busy.

That day we made love was the shit. I was eager to get inside her. She had the tightest pussy I'd experienced in a long time, and I lost all control. Maybe I rushed her; maybe I didn't take my time. Whatever it was, I needed to know. I saw she was going to make a brother work for her. I was going to have to pull out all the stops and was prepared to do just that. Maybe it was because I didn't eat the pussy. *Some women are just that shallow.* I ain't eating nobody's stuff but my wife's.

Now I hadn't always been that way, but with all these diseases and things that were going around, I had to be safe and selective. Plus, I was used to getting served, not me being the server. She'd better recognize who was sweating her. There were tons of honeys that would've liked a piece of this chocolate man. *I'll give her one more chance. Okay, maybe a couple of more chances.*

First chance
Second chance

One and only time
Yours and mine
Will it be?
I ask
I want to know
Putting on my battling gloves
Not willing to let you go

RELIVING THE PAST

Wesley was chilling with Czar, who asked him, "Where did you find that Layla chick? Are there any more like her?" He thought she was nice as hell and had a killer personality.

The little time they spent talking at the bar, he knew that she was exceptional. The other females Wesley normally brought around were stuck-up and out to be seen. They were either trying to be a singer or an actress—and some would settle for being a video ho—but with this Layla girl, he could tell this wasn't the case. She didn't have that star-struck, that "look-at-me, aren't-I-beautiful" vibe and attitude. She was one hundred percent natural.

"Why do you want to know?" Wesley knew they had the same taste in women and planned on keeping this one for himself. He still didn't know how he was going to get her.

"I was just curious."

"Well, don't be. I met her at the gym. She just moved here from Jersey and she's a writer—that's all the information you need to know, so leave it alone." Wesley felt threatened.

Czar just shook his head and ignored him.

You see, in Brooklyn, where they grew up, they shared many women, passing them back and forth. That was the nature of the drug game—the drug game and the "dog" game. Sell all the drugs you can sell, make all the money you can make, fuck all the pussy you can fuck, get your dick sucked as many times as you can—it was that simple. You either stuck to them, or you got caught up out there.

Wesley had been dealing drugs since the age of twelve. The lure of the money was what got him, not that his family was poor. His father worked for New York Transit, and his mother was a stylist for various artists, actors, and musicians. He did what he did on the down low, starting off as a runner for his sister's boyfriend, Self, the neighborhood kingpin.

"Stay away from him," his sister would warn him, when she threatened to tell their father.

But he didn't listen. Eventually he started holding, then selling. When his father found out, all hell broke loose. He kicked him out the house, telling him if he was man enough to sell drugs and put his life and their household in jeopardy, then he was old enough to get the hell out and be on his own.

Self put him up in an apartment, and all was good . . . until Self got shot and killed while leaving his house. That was enough to scare Wesley into turning his life around.

He'd been on enough assignments with his mom—video shoots, movie sets—to know that entertainment was where he wanted to be. There was a well-known producer who brought cocaine from him on a regular, and when Wesley expressed interest in the field, he became his mentor. When the drugs began to wear him down, he blamed it on the industry, entered rehab, and sold the company to Wesley, who, by then, had saved up a large percentage of his drug money.

The decision to bring the business to California was almost immediate. Wesley hired some people to run the business in New York, traveling there at least twice a month. Record sales were up for all his artists, and he soon became a millionaire.

The streets
Danger
Lurks on every block
Or cement
You stop on
Dipping and dodging
Won't help
Does no good
Getting out
Moving on
Hoping you could

SHE'S FINALLY HERE

The day finally came for Keke to arrive. I was like a kid in a candy store. I felt like I was about to have my first sleep-over. I couldn't wait to see my girl. I was walking out the house, ready to leave, when Quassmirah pulled up in her Lexus. *What the hell is she doing here?* If there was one thing I couldn't stand was when people showed up uninvited. *What if I was busy? What if I didn't feel like being bothered?* I almost walked back into the house and closed the door, but she spotted me.

She walked down the driveway. "Hey, girl, what's up?"

"Nothing. About to run to the airport." I closed the door behind me, hoping she'd get the hint.

"Really? Want me to ride with you?"

Now I knew she was bugging. I wasn't trying to have any-one come with me; I wanted Keke all to myself. We had a lot of catching up to do. "I don't think so."

Because of the hurt look on her face, I explained that I was going to pick up my best friend and wanted time alone with her.

"Oh, I understand," she replied, the disappointment obvi-ous in her voice.

"Maybe we can all hang out tomorrow." *Guilt will make you say and do some crazy things.*

"Oh, okay."

We headed towards the cars. "Well, call me," she said.

"I will—tomorrow," I told her, not even pretending like I would do it today.

The ride to the airport took over an hour. Traffic was backed up as usual. Kavan told me I should send a car, but I wanted to pick her up personally, go out to eat before coming home.

Standing in the terminal, I was bored as hell. There was security everywhere. It was announced that Keke's flight was delayed, so I decided to go into one of those little shopping areas and look around. I purchased the novel, *You Are Not Alone: a story of love, lust, and addiction,* by Angel Hunter.

Sitting down, I pulled out a book I'd brought along in case the flight was late—*Callus on My Soul,* the autobiography of Dick Gregory. Now I knew I shouldn't be reading stuff like this because I get caught up in it and, then become angry at the white man and all the injustices that were done to our people. Don't get it twisted, I wasn't one to walk around and say, "The white man this, the white man that . . ." But I just couldn't take certain books and movies.

Being a fan of Mr. Gregory's, I must have been engrossed in the book because the next thing you know, I felt someone tapping me on the shoulder. I turned around, and there stood Keke. I jumped out my seat and hugged her tight against me. "Oh my God, girl, I missed you so much," I gushed, almost in tears.

It felt so good to see her. I missed having her around to laugh with, to cry with; to share my joys, my fears, and my doubts. Yes, we called each other on the phone, but that was nothing compared to physical interaction. When you had a friend who knew your mood just by the sound of your voice, it was something precious. A friend that you could piss off, curse out, and act ignorant towards and they still loved you.

"I missed you too."

We stepped back and took a long look at one another to see if anything had changed.

"Don't say it." She laughed. "I've put on some weight."

I did notice it, but I wouldn't have said it to her. "I could barely tell," I lied.

She gave me a "yeah, right" look.

I just laughed.

Keke was wearing a jean suit, a baby doll T-shirt, and sported a baseball cap.

"What's up with the baseball cap?" I asked on our way to get her bags.

"Well . . ." She pulled it off.

Homegirl was locking her hair. "Oh my God," I said. Not that I didn't like it, I was just thrown for a loop. You see, Keke loved her perms, and the straighter the better.

"Surprise!" She laughed at the expression on my face.

"And a surprise it is." I reached for her hair and touched it.

"What do you think?"

I stood back and examined her from head to toe. I loved it. It fit her face, made her cheekbones protrude, and opened her eyes. But I wanted to tease her a little, so I frowned.

"You don't think it's me, do you?" She sounded so upset.

I decided to be honest. "I love it."

"You do?"

"Yes, I do. You look almost regal."

"I do, don't I?"

"What made you start locking your hair? And why didn't you tell me sooner?"

"See, I knew you didn't like it."

"No, I do, it's just that I'm in shock. You know how you are, girl, not a hair ever out of place. You stayed in the hairdresser's. Shit, you even had your own chair. This is a big decision. Why now?"

"It's a change, girl—that and the ease of it. Going to the hairdresser's, touching up my roots, putting all that shit in my hair, was taking its toll; plus I felt like the chemicals were soaking into my brain or something."

I started laughing. "Well, I like it, and I'm proud of you."

"I'm proud of myself. It makes me feel like the queen I am and less artificial."

We were at luggage claim waiting for her bags, when I decided to ask her, "So, have you seen Jaye lately?"

"I was wondering how long it was going to take you to ask me about him. I saw him before I left and he told me to give you this." She reached in her bag and pulled out a folder.

I took it from her. "Kind of thick, don't ya think?"

She shrugged her shoulders and grabbed a couple of bags off the track.

I asked her, "Wanna grab something to eat?"

"Girl, I'm tired and hungry. I'd like to shower and take a nap first."

"Fine by me," I said, disappointed.

We were headed towards the car, when she asked me if Kavan was home.

"He's on the set today, shooting his new movie."

She and Kavan weren't as tight as he and I, but they were good friends.

I thought we would talk on the way home, but no such luck—Keke fell asleep as soon as we hit the freeway. I wanted to wake her up, but decided to let her rest.

When we pulled into the driveway I nudged her awake. She opened her eyes, took one look at the house, and said, "Holy shit!"

I just laughed.

As soon as we walked in the house, the phone rang. I rushed to pick it up. "Hello?"

"Hey, sweetie," Wesley said, "are you busy?"

"Yes, my best friend is here from Jersey. I just came in from the airport."

"What are y'all doing tonight?"

"Chillin'."

"Want to come to a party with me?"

I almost said no, because like I told Quassmirah, Keke's first day here was for us to play catch up, but I also knew that when Wesley said a party, it meant an industry party, and Keke would like that—being around celebrities; plus, I wanted to show off a little. "I don't know. Let me discuss it with her and I'll call you back."

"Make sure you do that."

I turned around to ask Keke about the party and she was nowhere in sight. "Keke!" I went in search of her. As I turned the corner, we bumped right into each other.

"This house is the shit! Oh my God, Layla, Kavan is doing his thing."

I laughed because her reaction was the same as mine when I first saw it. Taking her hand and leaving the bags on the floor, I told her, "Come on, let's go upstairs to your room."

"My room?"

"Yes, you'll have your own private room."

"Oh." She sounded disappointed.

"Why you say, 'oh,' like that?"

"I thought we were going to do like we used to—stay together in the same room, kind of like a sleepover."

I started laughing. She took me back to being a teenager, when we would stay the night over each other's house on Friday nights. If I wasn't at hers, she was at mine. It didn't matter, as long as we were together. If we weren't together, we were on the phone for hours at a time.

"Didn't you two just see each other in school? What do you have to talk about?" our parents would ask.

We had a lot to talk about: From boys, to boys, to more boys.

We were so close that if we got into trouble together and our parents told us we couldn't go over one another's house, or even if we didn't get into trouble and they just felt like we needed a break from one another, we'd write letters to each other and have my brothers pass them along—for a nominal fee of course.

"I'd like that. I just thought that since we were older, you'd think it was corny."

"Girl, please . . . I love you, and you're never too old for a sleepover."

I hugged her. "I love you too. Let's go to our room then."

We grabbed her bags and walked up the stairs. I opened the bedroom door slowly, knowing she would love it—purple was her favorite color, and the color theme in my room was purple and gold.

Placing her hand on her breast, she exclaimed, "This is the shit!"

"I know, right? Kavan has such excellent taste that I didn't have to change a thing; I just moved right in."

"Maybe I need to move in too."

I knew she was just talking, so I didn't say a word.

"So, what are we doing tonight?" She plopped down on the bed.

"I don't know. Wesley invited us to a party, but I was thinking we could just go out to dinner and talk."

"Wesley is that record producer guy you're seeing, right?"

"Yeah."

"You sure don't sound like you like him much."

"It's not that, it's just that he's so aggressive. He's calls me constantly. He doesn't give a sister a chance to even miss him—not that I need to . . . because he's not my man."

"Well, you're a good woman. Maybe he sees that and is not trying to let you get by."

"I understand all that, but I'm not trying to be had by anyone."

Standing up and opening her bags, Keke said, "Well, if you

really don't feel like hanging with him tonight, we don't have to. I didn't come here to force you to do something you don't want to do, although it does sound like fun."

I have to admit a sister was torn. I wanted to say, "Good, then let's not go," but I couldn't do that to her. She flew all the way across the country to visit me, and I wanted to show her a good time. What better way than an industry party?

"Nah, we'll go." I pulled out a drawer and emptied it on the bed. "You can put your clothes in there. I'm going to go downstairs and see what I can throw together for us to eat."

"I'm going to take a shower, then lay down for an hour, okay?"

"Okay."

I went downstairs into the kitchen and opened the freezer. Not really in the mood to cook, I pulled out Stouffer's veggie lasagna. (It was as delicious as the real thing.)

I sat down to call Wesley on his personal line.

"Hello."

"Hi, Wesley."

"Hey, gorgeous."

"Do you know who you're talking to?"

"Of course. What do you think?—I call everyone gorgeous?"

I just laughed.

"So what's up? You and your girl coming to the party or what?"

"Yes, we're going."

"Good. I'm glad to hear that. I'll send a car for you around 11 p.m."

I was glad he suggested it. "You don't have to do that."

"I know I don't have to; I want to."

What was there left to say other than, "Thank you?"

"Oh, and bring that singer girl with you. I have someone I want her to meet."

I didn't feel like hanging with Quassmirah, but I couldn't tell him no. "Well, I'll see you tonight," I told him.

"A'ight. Peace."

I went upstairs to check on Keke. She was wrapped up in a towel. "I just put some lasagna in the oven."

"You made it that quick?"

"Stouffer's made it."

"I know that's right." She laughed.

"I spoke to Wesley about us going out with him. He's going to send a car at 11, so go ahead and lay down. I need to work on this script I'm writing for class."

"All right. Don't let me sleep too long."

"I won't," I told her and went to call Quassmirah.

A best friend
To hold your hand
Touch your heart
Share in laughter
Wipe your tears
Throughout the years
Always understanding

QUASSMIRAH

*H*omegirl *must have it going on.* She lives with the comedian Kavan, and Wesley Jones is trying to press up. Damn, some bitches have all the luck. I'd been out here for three years now, hadn't met anyone to take me to the next level; been dogged out one too many times. Sometimes I just felt like giving up. I'd done a couple of commercials that helped pay the bills, and did a few jingles, nothing major. *Maybe my luck is about to change.* I was feeling this new energy, and maybe if I applied it right, Layla might hook me up with Wesley.

When she called to invite me along, I decided to make the most of this opportunity. Not only was I going to look fierce, but I was going to work my charms on every single person, male or female, that I came into contact with.

IT'S PARTY TIME

As the car Wesley sent pulled up, Kavan walked through the door and looked at all three. "Well, well, well, what do we have here?"

Smiling, Keke ran up to him and kissed him on the cheek.

"So you finally made it." He kissed her back.

"Yep, and I'm loving it already."

He looked at Quassmirah. "Who is this young lady?"

Not waiting for an introduction, she reached her hand out. "I'm Quassmirah, and the pleasure is mine."

"Are you an actress?"

"That, and a singer."

"Are you from here?"

"I've been here three years now."

Not one to beat around the bush, Kavan told her, "Take care of my friends out there. I trust them with no one other than myself."

"I will," Quassmirah said. She didn't know what else to say—he threw her off, being so blunt.

"Okay," Layla said, "enough of the father stuff, Kavan."

"I'm just looking out." He looked at Quassmirah. "Just remember what I said."

Layla rolled her eyes. "Come on. Let's go before he locks us in."

Kavan watched them walk out the door.

Once in the car, Quassmirah asked Layla, "Is he always like that?"

"Like what?"

"Forward."

"When it comes to those he loves?"

"It's a damn shame he's gay; brother is fine."

"So, tell me . . . how long have you two been friends?" Quassmirah asked. "You got any brothers or sisters? What made you move out here? Do you do anything besides teach at the gym?"

The last time they'd gotten together, Quassmirah did the majority of the talking, mostly about men, with neither revealing too much of themselves.

Nosey, aren't we? Layla thought. "How about you tell me about yourself first?"

Now that was something Quassmirah didn't want to do. Her life had been one of poverty, hopelessness, and instability. It was something she was ashamed of and embarrassed about— growing up in the hood. For as long as she could remember her family was on welfare. There were four kids in the family—she had three older brothers—and all four of them had different fathers. She was the youngest. Her mother was a drug addict. It was not a secret to any of them. They were taunted as kids, picked on, and embarrassed day in and day out.

Quassmirah recalled wearing hand-me-down clothes from the Salvation Army and one day going to school only to find out that she had on another student's gear. Talk about embarrassed. She cut school for a whole week. Her mother found out and gave her a beating that left scars on her legs. She even made Quassmirah go out and pick the switch from the tree.

Quassmirah didn't know how attractive she was until she became a teenager. When she hit the ninth grade, all of a sudden she was getting attention from boys. So much so, she didn't know what to do; it frightened her. Until she met Chris.

To this day, when she thought about Chris, it stirred up emotions. He was her first love. He was also a drug dealer. He had a thick build, wore a lot of jewelry, was flashy, drove a BMW, and already had a girl. Quassmirah would see him almost every day on her way home from school. She knew he was watching her and wondered why he never said a word to her. One day when she arrived home, he was sitting in the living room with her brother, cutting up cocaine.

"Y'all want something to eat?" she asked. She'd read in *Cosmopolitan* magazine that the way to a man's heart was through his stomach. There was one thing she knew she could do, and that was cook. She cooked for her brothers all the time.

"Yeah," her brother said.

She cooked some steak, mashed potatoes, and fried corn. After that, Chris would stop by almost every day, eat dinner and just hang out, striking up conversation with her. Her brothers knew what was going on, but decided it wasn't causing anyone harm.

Finally, Chris asked her out for her sixteenth birthday. They went to dinner and a movie. After the movie, he asked her, "You ready to go home?"

"No. I want to go to your house." She was ready to lose her virginity and wanted him to be the one.

He took her home and made love to her like she was a woman. She was hooked. She thought he was going to be the one she married. The one who would rescue her. But it didn't happen. He was killed in a car accident.

Quassmirah found out in school. She received a page from her brother 911. She left school and walked to her house in a daze, only to find her mother in the kitchen on the floor. She wanted to call the police, social services, someone—anyone. But there were drugs on the table, and it would only mean trouble. Feeling a heartbeat, she dragged her mother to the couch and put a cold rag on her face, and vowed to leave home as soon as possible. It was just one tragedy after another.

There were plenty of times when she wanted to call social services, the cops, somebody, but she didn't because they would be put in foster homes. And that would mean splitting them up.

Her older brother dropped out of school and did what he had to do to take care of her and her younger brothers. They just let their mother exist.

Living under those conditions made Quassmirah an over-achiever. She wanted to be the best at everything. She wanted more and more and would do anything to get it, thinking material things would make her happy.

After hearing how beautiful she was over and over, she knew she wanted to be in the world of entertainment. She tried to convince her brothers to allow her to quit school and pursue modeling, but they weren't hearing it. As a matter of fact, they made her go to college, where she majored in the-ater and communication. Two days after graduation, she found herself in California, chasing her dream of riches and fame—no matter what the cost.

"Well?" Layla was still waiting on a reply.

"There's not much to tell," Quassmirah told her. "I'm from Washington, DC; Chocolate City. I have three brothers, and well, that's my story."

> *My past is just that*
> *To be left behind*
> *Not retraced*

Unknown
I prefer non-existent
Focus on the me
Now
The present

PARTY TIME

When we pulled up to the club, the line to get in was ridiculously long. Thank God, we were on the guest list. The bouncers at the door were handpicking which women would get in the club.

Climbing out the car, I glanced over at Keke, who was wearing a tailored black pants suit that was tapered at the leg. Her V-neck jacket stopped just below her cleavage, which she was proudly showing, killing the push up bra, stopped mid-behind, and had no collar. I smiled at the "I-belong-here" look on her face.

Quassmirah went all out in her black unitard leather jumper that looked like it was poured on her and showed off every curve in her skinny body. She looked like the singer she wanted to become. *Do it, girl.*

I was looking just as good in my long white dress, which fit my curves, left my back exposed. I had my hair pulled up and some small studs in my ears. Yes, us three ladies were ready to party.

Wesley left instructions with the driver for me to call him on his cell once we were outside the club. I dialed the number.

"Speak," he said, the music blasting in the background.

"Hey, it's me. We're outside in front."

"I'll send my boy out to get you. Sit tight."

"Okay."

"What's up? Are we going in or what?" Quassmirah asked anxiously.

I'd made the mistake of telling her in advance that Wesley wanted her to meet someone.

Keke looked at me and rolled her eyes. The second she met Quassmirah I knew she didn't like her. She barely said ten words to the girl.

"Wesley is sending someone to escort us in."

We must have waited for five minutes and in that short span of time, Horace Brown, Suge Knight, and a few other well-known musical geniuses walked in with their entourages.

Someone knocked on the window. I was pleased to see Czar.

He opened the door and smiled. "Hey there."

"Hi." I kissed him on the cheek, surprising us both. I stepped to the side and introduced Keke as she got out the car. He already knew Quassmirah from the club.

"Follow me, ladies."

When we walked in the club, I almost said, "Wow!" out loud. It was all that and then some. The color scheme was burgundy and gold. There were dancers on the stage and in cages. I had never been to a place like this before. I looked to the right and saw stairs leading up and down. I asked Czar, "How many floors are in here?"

"Three. This is the main floor, which plays R&B and hip-hop. The bottom floor plays jazz and upstairs is VIP, which plays a little of everything."

We headed towards the stairs.

"Of course, we're going to VIP," Quassmirah said, all smiles.

"Of course," Czar replied.

People were watching us as we walked by. A few women stopped Czar and asked him if they could follow us. I even heard a few ask if Wesley was around, but Czar blew them off.

When we got upstairs, I spotted Wesley right away, sitting at a crowded table. He spotted me at the same time and winked.

"Thanks for being our escort," I told Czar.

"My pleasure." He took my hand and kissed it and went back downstairs.

"I don't think Wesley liked that too much," Quassmirah whispered.

"Liked what?"

"The kissing of the hand."

I looked at Wesley and hoped I was reading him wrong. He did look pissed, but by the time I reached him, his frown was a smile.

He stood up and hugged me before extending his hand out to Keke. "So, you're the famous best friend; I've heard a lot about you."

"Good things, I hope."

I looked at Wesley. I didn't recall mentioning Keke to him.

He looked at Quassmirah and smiled. "Don't you look like a tigress tonight!"

Of course, she took it all in.

"Have a seat."

We sat next to him on the couch, although what I wanted to do was dance. They were playing DMX, and I was feeling it. It had been a while since I'd been out and I wanted to party, even though at first I didn't want to come at all.

Wesley asked each of us if we would like something to drink, and of course, we said yes. While we were waiting on our drinks, we people-watched, and when we got tired of that, Keke suggested we walk around.

"Wesley, we're going to walk around, okay," I told him.

"You're sure? You want one of my boys to come with you?"

"No, Keke would like to see the whole club, not just the VIP area."

"I'm going to stay here," Quassmirah said.

That was fine by me. I knew she wanted to network. Keke and I grabbed our drinks, and off we went.

"Where did you meet her?" Keke asked.

"At the gym."

"She's a character; be careful around her. There's something about her I just don't like."

"I will."

Keke was a good judge of character. If she said be careful around someone, it was best to listen. She had a sixth sense about people. It was always that way, and most of the time she was right.

"I'm serious."

"I know, I know."

When we got to the bottom of the stairs we bumped right into Czar. "Hey, cutie, Wesley actually let you out of his sight?"

"He doesn't own me," I said, meaning it but trying not to sound too harsh.

"I hear that." Stepping between me and Keke, he took both of our hands and said, "Let's dance."

We gladly did.

We partied our asses off. We drank, laughed, flirted, drank, and laughed some more.

I danced with Czar for quite some time and found him to be funny and a gentleman. I have to admit, we had a chemistry going on. I had to catch myself a couple of times and remind myself that he was Wesley's boy. No, we weren't a couple, but still, it was the principle of the matter.

After about the fifth song, Czar said he was tired, so I started dancing with someone else. Two minutes into the song, the brother started violating my space, getting a bit closer than I appreciated. That was something I couldn't stand—*Why do men think that just because you give them a dance or two, they have a license to press up? If I can feel your dick, there's a problem; if I can smell your breath, there's a problem; if I can smell your body odor, that's definitely a problem.*

Anyway, I put my hands on his chest to push him back, and he held them there.

"What are you doing?" I snatched my hands away. "I was trying to back you up, not get closer."

He had the audacity to put his hands on my hips and say, "Aw, come on, baby."

Before I could reply, Czar was standing between us. "What's going on here?"

"Who are you?—her fuckin' bodyguard?"

"I will be, if I have to."

Scared that things were going to get out of hand, I stepped up. "Czar, don't worry about him; we're finished dancing anyway."

Czar stood in the guy's face. "I'd advise you to step off."

The next thing you know, Wesley was standing behind us. He appeared from out of nowhere. "Is there a problem?"

"Nah, nah, there's no problem." Just like that he walked away, with Wesley and Czar watching his every move.

When he was no longer in sight, they both turned towards me and asked, "You okay?"

"I'm fine." I glanced at my watch and told Wesley, "I'm almost ready to go home."

"It's still early. We haven't even spent time together. Why don't you and your girl come stay the night at my house tonight? I have extra rooms."

Now, I knew he was bugging. "I don't think so. I think Keke would rather stay her first night with me alone."

"I understand. Just stay a little while longer. Give me five minutes, and all my attention will be devoted to you, I promise."

I didn't really care if all his attention was devoted to me or not. I came out to show Keke a good time, not to be on a date. Of course I didn't tell him that.

Just then, Keke and the finest mocha-toned brother I'd seen in life walked up. She was holding his hand. "Layla, meet my new friend, James."

He put out his hand for me to shake.

"Nice to meet you," I told him, smiling at Keke, trying to let her know that she'd won the prize.

"Well, we'll be upstairs getting to know one another better. Let me know when you're ready to leave."

With a smile on his face, Wesley said, "It doesn't look like you'll be leaving any time soon."

"I'll check you two later," Czar said; "it's too many honeys up in here to be standing in one place."

Before he could walk off, Wesley asked him if he wouldn't mind keeping me company for five more minutes.

"You don't have to," I told him. "I'm a grown woman. I can take care of myself."

"Oh, I don't mind." he replied, and just that quick, Wesley was off.

Wesley was gone for exactly five minutes, and in that time, me and Czar had become friends somewhat. I learned that he was from Brooklyn as well and owned the bar that we were in. He was single with no kids. I have to admit, I liked him. I liked him a lot. Kind of wished I'd met him first and that's probably why that night as I lay in bed, my thoughts were so consumed with him. I dreamed we kissed—the messed up part about it was where we were—Wesley's house.

I was in Wesley's kitchen cooking when Czar came up behind me and said, "You are so beautiful."

"Thanks."

He put his hands around my waist, pressed up against me,

and said, "I want to kiss you, I want to taste you, I want to feel you."

Unable to say no, I turned around and told him, "Then do it—kiss me, taste me, feel me."

He brought his lips down to mine and pressed them gently against his, not opening his mouth, but gently rubbing his lips against mine. He then parted my mouth with his tongue and ran it in the middle. "Stick out your tongue."

I did, and he took my tongue in his mouth and sucked on it gently.

I felt my vagina getting moist. The dream felt so real, I must have moaned out loud because Keke pushed me out of my sleep.

"What or, shall I say, who were you dreaming about?"

"Girl, you wouldn't believe me if I told you; I don't believe it myself."

"I know you better tell, since your ass woke me up moaning and groaning."

I laughed. "Wesley's friend, Czar."

"Yeah?" Instead of joking about it, like I thought she would, she told me, "You be careful, girl—Wesley doesn't look like the type to share."

"Damn! It was just a dream."

"Yeah, but dreams have a way of coming true."

Keke's visit confirmed what I already knew—I missed home. We partied so much while she was here. It was like we were teenagers. We even ran into Czar and ended up hanging with him the whole night. This time Kavan was with us.

When the evening was over, Kavan asked, "What's up with you and him?"

"What do you mean, what's up with us?—Nothing; he's a friend of Wesley's."

"I don't know, girl. I felt some kind of vibe thing happening between the two of you."

Keke looked at me with a raised eyebrow. I know she was thinking of the dream I had.

"Kavan, please . . . you're just trying to make something out of nothing."

He just rolled his eyes at me.

Later that night I found myself thinking about Czar and how attentive he was with us, buying us drinks, making sure we had a good time and were treated like VIP.

I took his number, but not to go out or anything. He just made me feel real comfortable, made me feel like he'd be a good friend, and I figured you could never have too many of them.

When the day arrived for Keke to leave, we cried like babies. I made her promise that she'd come visit again soon.

"Girl, wild dogs couldn't keep me away."

"Wild dogs or that fine-ass brother you met?"

"Wild dogs, the fine-ass brother, as you say, and my friendship with you—how's that for an answer?"

"Can't think of a better one." *Damn! I'm going to miss her.*

> *Goodbye is never easy*
> *Even if it's for a short while*
> *You wonder*
> *Will I see you again*
> *Will we talk*
> *Will I be missed*
> *In a way*
> *It's letting go*
> *Of the moment*

THE MEETING

It had been a couple of weeks since Keke left, and I'd been in a serious funk. I was home getting ready for a meeting with Wesley. I must have been moving slow because Kavan came into my room and said, "Girl, you're not acting like you want this opportunity."

"I do."

"Well, you need to get the move on."

I was meeting with Wesley and a video director. Wesley had a new girl group called Essence that was coming out with a new single and he wanted to hire me to come up with a concept for the video and to write a mini-script. The competition out there was so tough when it came to videos. They had become like mini-movies. So what I was going to do was meet the girls, listen to the song in their presence, get a feel for them, and pitch some ideas. When Wesley first approached me about doing this, I wasn't sure because I knew he was trying to make me his woman, and I didn't want to feel obligated to him or feel like I owed him anything. On the other hand, I knew that this was an opportunity.

I went back and forth with it so much and finally took the idea to Kavan. "Girl, do the damn video. Where you get your opportunity shouldn't matter; what's important is that you take advantage of it. Shit, just make it clear to him that no strings are attached, that this does not mean that you'll be giving up the booty, that's it strictly a business thing."

Prior to the meeting, Wesley and I had lunch. Maybe I was jumping ahead of the game, making rules and laying the down the law before I even got the job. The way I figured it, I might as well, because that way he'd know where I stood before we even began.

We agreed to meet at the "Juice Bar." When I walked in, I glanced around and found Wesley standing at the counter. He waved me over. "Hey there."

"Hey yourself." He kissed me on the cheek, and I followed him to a table. We sat down and looked at the menus.

We didn't talk about much of anything until after the waitress came over and we placed our orders.

"Are you excited about the meeting?" he asked.

"Yes, that's what I wanted to talk to you about—if I get the job, what does it mean?"

"What do you mean, 'what does it mean?'—it means you get the job."

"That's not what I'm talking about."

He looked genuinely puzzled. For a minute there I almost said, "Forget it," because I was starting to feel stupid, like I was blowing this out of proportion.

I could hear Kavan saying, "Better safe than sorry."

"If you offer me the job, I hope it's not because you want something in return." I saw in his eyes that he was finally getting what I was saying.

"Oh, you think I asked you in on this so that I can get the ass again?"

"I just want to make it clear that it's business only. That it won't interfere with our rela—that it won't interfere with our friendship and that we'll be able to keep it separate."

"Girl, I've been in this business for quite some time. I don't get down like that. I know you need a break, and I'm in the

position to give you one—that's what this is about. Not me trying to win you over, or me trying to get the ass."

I looked at him, feeling a little relieved. "Okay."

We ordered our food and started to eat.

There was still tension in the air, and I wanted to get past it.
"Are you mad at me?"

"Nah, baby, I ain't mad at you. A little surprised that you
would even think something like that. Although it makes a
brother feel good to know that you're looking out for yourself; that you're not going to allow anyone to take advantage
of you. It just pains me to know you would even think I'm that
type of brother."

"I'm sorry if I insulted you."

He didn't say anything. We finished eating, and I followed
him to the office.

Did I hurt your feelings
Did I let you down
Did I do to you
What I'd hate to be done to me
Did I tear you apart
Or were they just words
In one ear and out the other
Should I apologize
Or let it go
Please let me know

WESLEY

I played that shit off good as hell. Of course I wanted something in return. What did she think this was? Nothing was free in the entertainment world. And the sooner she realized that, the better off she was going to be. Her girl Quassmirah—she knew the deal, and because of that I got her singing background on one of my artist's albums—homegirl sucked a mean dick.

You might think I was foul, but I wasn't. I was just a brother who liked to get his dick sucked. I didn't make her do it. I didn't even come on to her. Okay, I could have told her no, but why? I didn't have a woman. I was trying to make Layla my woman, but what she didn't know couldn't hurt her.

I was positive Quassmirah wasn't going to tell her. Plus, Layla wasn't giving me any pussy.

The night at the club when Layla's friend was visiting from Jersey, Quassmirah and I had a chance to talk. I'd heard her voice but had yet to sit down and kick it with her. You see, before I worked with an artist, I needed to know what they were about. There were a lot of artists out there with some fucked up personalities who I refused to deal with. I liked my musical family to have a certain flow, and that was one of ease and comfort.

She wasn't Whitney or anything, but she had that star quality. After talking to her, I found out she had personality as well. She wasn't as stuck up as a lot of these other women in L.A.

I introduced her around to a few producers and told her to come to the studio the following Monday. I wasn't planning on anything. I just wanted her to listen to some material. That Monday when she arrived, I should have steered clear because she was giving me the look the whole time. I knew I was a good catch, but I was also seeing her girl.

I had her singing background on a slow, sexy rap joint titled "What I Like." It was about a brother saying what he wanted from a woman in and out of bed. Her part went something like this:

I'll give you what you want
Your every desire
I'll make you moan my name in pleasure
Call you king or sire

Now the lyrics may not have been all that, but the way she sang them was. She had a lot of what we were looking for—attitude.

When the studio session was over, she told me she wanted to speak with me in private, so we went into my office. She closed the door behind her.

"What's up?"

"I just wanted to thank you for giving me this opportunity."

"Well, you have an interesting sound and an exotic look. When we get ready to do the video, you'll get even more exposure."

"Guess its true what they say about being in the right place at the right time and who you know." As she was talking to me, I noticed that she started to get closer and closer.

"So tell me, what's up with you and Layla? Are you dating

each other exclusively?" By now, she was standing directly in front of me.

Mind you, I was sitting down, so when she sat on the desk in that short-ass skirt she was wearing, I did what any healthy man would do—take a quick peek between her legs.

When she saw me looking, she opened them slightly.

Homegirl wasn't wearing any panties.

"You like what you see?"

I knew I should have got up and walked out. "Yeah, I like what I see."

In a very seductive tone, she asked, "Do you want what you see?"

Now I got offered sex often, so it wasn't any big deal. I told her, "Sometimes what I like and what I want are two different things."

She jumped off the desk and asked me again, "So what's up with you and Layla?"

"Nothing. We're just kicking it."

Still standing in front of me, she said, "I want to repay you for your kindness."

"You will . . . by helping to promote the record."

"I want to repay you in a more personal way."

The next thing I know, she was on her knees, and my dick was out my pants quicker than a speeding bullet. I was about to stop her, but once I felt her tongue lick the shaft of my "johnson" like it was the best lollipop in the world, there was nothing I could do.

I leaned back in the chair and let her go to work. I closed my eyes and pretended it was Layla—till I reached the point of no return.

While she was working that mouth, I pulled open my drawer and took out some paper towels; I was about to come.

When all was said and done, I wiped myself off, looked at her, and said, "This will stay between us."

"Of course."

An awkward silence filled the room.

Finally I stood up. As we walked out together, Czar was on the other side of the door, about to knock.

"I'll see you later?"

"All right," I told her and watched her walk away.

Czar was watching me watch her. "What's up with her?"

"Nothing. She's working on Devine's album."

"She's Layla's friend, right?"

Czar wasn't stupid. He could feel something was up.

> *Sometimes we do things*
> *For no reason at all*
> *Not meaning*
> *To hurt another*
> *Sometimes we say*
> *What we feel*
> *Not meaning what we say*
> *After a thought or two*
> *What's a person to do?*
> *Apologize?*

A COINCIDENCE

"So what do you think, Layla?" Wesley asked. We were meeting in his office. I'd listened to the song a number of times and met with the girls and had already formulated a few ideas.

"I want to tell the story of the song, scene by scene, but the thing is, since a video is but so long, the verbal part of each scene has to come before the chorus, and be one or two powerful lines."

I threw around some more ideas and told him I would go home and write up a couple of treatments and get them to him in two days.

"Can I see you tonight?" he asked. "To celebrate us doing business together?"

I looked at him. I didn't know why I was giving this brother such a hard way to go. Here, he was helping a sister to advance—he'd been nothing but respectful and kind to me—and I kept kicking him to the curb. *Maybe I'll give him a chance.*

I hadn't heard from Jaye, other than once. When I returned his call, he didn't call me back. The package he sent through Keke was pictures of us in a scrapbook. I was still trying to figure out why he sent that. Keke said he asked about me all the time. My mother said he came by to check on her, and my brothers said he looked depressed. *Well, good for his ass.*

"Yes, we can go out and celebrate."

"I'll pick you up around 8 p.m."

You would think he just won the lottery, with the smile plastered on his face. As he stood up, his intercom beeped. He picked up the phone.

"You don't have to walk me down. I'll see you later."

I walked out the office, dead smack into TC, Kavan's man. I was surprised to see him. "TC, what are you doing here?" I went to give him a hug and felt him tighten up.

"I'm doing a song for Wesley. What are you doing here?"

He looked nervous as he stood there. I was about to ask him if everything was okay, and then I remembered that his sexuality was a secret in the music industry.

"You don't have to worry about me saying anything."

Relief flooded his face.

I turned to walk away but stopped when he called my name.

"Yes?"

"Thanks," he said.

Secrets can rape you
Break you
Or take you out
Why are you keeping them
What's that all about

TC

Imagine my astonishment running into Layla. Shit, I was as surprised to see her as she was to see me. Actually, I was flabbergasted because I felt busted, like I was about to be found out. I had no idea she was in the music industry. I knew that Kavan said she was a writer, I just never thought that our paths would cross. Now that they did, I was a little nervous about it—she knew that I swung both ways. Correction—she knew I was gay. I'd been in denial for so long, and in a way, still was. I was in the closet.

I worked mostly with the hip-hop industry and everyone was hardcore. In order to survive and to continue getting the same clientele, I had to be "heterosexual." Dr. Jekyll and Mr. Hyde, I was. A man that lived two lives. It was difficult, and I didn't know how much longer I was going to be able to do it.

On top of everything else, I found myself falling in love with Kavan. I wanted to be a couple out in the open, but was afraid of the backlash. Nonetheless, when she said she wouldn't tell I almost started to cry, because it was a shame I had to keep my lifestyle a damn secret.

I was headed to Wesley's office when I heard him laugh and say into the speakerphone, "Quassmirah, now you know that's not possible."

"Why? You and Layla aren't serious."

Layla? Who was this Quassmirah chick? And why was she talking about Layla to Wesley? I decided to listen a little more.

"That's not the point. The point is we made a mistake—you're her friend, for goodness sake."

"Didn't it feel good to you?"

"That it did."

"I can do other things that feel just as good."

Shit, I wish I could see Wesley's face and this so-called friend of Layla's. I'm telling Kavan about this. Layla is his girl and she will not get played.

When I'd heard enough, I knocked on his door.

Wesley saw me and picked up the phone. "One of my producers is here. Don't forget the studio session tomorrow." He hung up the phone. Shaking his head, he looked at me with a smirk. "Women . . . always want what they can't have."

"It sounded to me like she had you already." I was fishing for information.

"Maybe, maybe not—I don't kiss and tell. Have a seat."

"The walls will come crashing down," I said to myself, looking at him with disdain.

What's done in the dark
Will come out
No need to run
No place to hide
Rules
Unspoken laws
The light is coming soon

THE CALL I'D BEEN WAITING ON

When I arrived home, I went straight to the room and picked up the phone to see retrieve my messages.

Layla, this is Jaye. He hesitated. *I miss you. Call me so we can talk.*

I must have sat still and looked at the phone for a good two minutes, collecting my thoughts. I was surprised he called and now that he had, I wasn't sure what I would say when I called him back. *What is there to talk about?* If it's us, there's nothing more to be said. But then again, he also said he missed me. That made me feel good. Gave me a warm feeling.

I dialed the number I'd known by heart almost all my life. Jaye answered on the second ring.

"Jaye, it's Layla." My heart was racing.

"Layla, I see you got my message. How's L.A. treating you?"

"It's okay."

"Just okay?"

Well, what the hell did he want me to say—that it was wonderful, that I was having the time of my life? "Yes, okay."

"Have you met anyone yet?"

"Why do you care?—you've only called me once since I've been here."

"I sent a package with Keke."

"It's not the same."

"I was heartbroken."

"Well, so was I."

"You're the one who left."

"You know why I left—I had to get on with my life; I was tired of waiting around for you."

"So, you have met someone?"

"No, and I'm not looking to meet anyone. That's not why I moved here. Have you met anyone?"

"No one as special as you."

Neither of us said anything for a second or two.

"Do you miss me?" Jaye asked.

Now why he gotta go and ask me something like that? Of course, I missed his ass. He'd been in my life since the ninth grade. "Yes, I do, Jaye, but missing you is not enough."

"I was thinking about visiting you."

He surprised me with that one, but I surprised myself even more by saying, "Okay."

When Kavan arrived home that night, I told him Jaye was coming to visit in three weeks.

"Girl, are you crazy?"

"What? Why I gotta be crazy?"

"You know all he wants to do is make you change your mind and take you back to Jersey. He's a man; his ego and his pride is hurt—you up and left his ass. He's lonely and he realizes that he fucked up. Now he's bringing his ass all the way to California and will try to get you to change your focus."

Kavan was going off. He was pissed for real, and it made me smile that he cared so much.

I had this fantasy that when Jaye got here, he'd realize that he should move with me. After listening to Kavan, who wasn't done speaking his piece, I knew there was almost no chance of that happening.

"What are you going to do when Jaye begs and pleads, pulls

out the fat engagement ring and says he can't live without you, to please come home? What are you going to do then?"

"Well, he'll just get his feelings hurt then."

"You think so? What are you going to tell Wesley?"

"What do you mean, what am I going to tell Wesley?—Wesley ain't my man."

"Yeah, right. Homeboy has been taking you out, wining and dining you, showing you a good time for no reason at all—is that the lie you're telling yourself?"

"So what are you saying?"

"What I'm saying is, out of respect, you should tell him about Jaye. It's obvious you still have feelings for him, and when he gets here, you can't predict what will or won't take place."

I heard him, but I wasn't listening.

> *How will it go*
> *Will you leave*
> *Will you stay*
> *Will you break my heart*
> *Or make my day*
> *Will I be stranded*
> *With an ache*
> *I'm not sure how much I can take*

JAYE'S ARRIVAL

Lazy from the morning heat, I was in bed on the phone with Wesley. He wanted me to go to breakfast with him.

"I can't do that."

"Why not?"

"What do you mean, why not? If I tell you I can't go, I just can't."

"I want a reason."

Now my immediate response was to hang up on his ass. Talking 'bout he want a reason. *Well, I'll give him a reason, and it'll be one he won't like.*

"I have a friend coming from Jersey, and he's arriving today."

"He's arriving?"

I didn't take Kavan's advice and tell him about Jaye previously. "Yes, *he.*"

"Oh, I see. Is this a friend or a boyfriend?"

"It's a friend."

"Well, how about we all get together?"

"I don't think so."

"You don't think so?"

"No."

"So it's like that?"

"Wesley, why are you tripping? I told you I'm having company and I want to spend time with my company. How about I call you once he leaves?"

"Do that," he said and hung up.

I don't have time for this shit. I had more important things to do, like get ready for Jaye. I wasn't picking him up from the airport.

"Don't go all out for him; don't act anxious," Kavan said. "He's the one who didn't do right by you—make him sweat you."

I didn't know about all that. I wasn't a "game-player."

I showered and put on a jean mini-skirt with a baby T, for a look that was sexy, casual, and comfortable. I may have looked at ease, but wasn't feeling it at all.

No matter how nonchalant I tried to act, I was nervous about Jaye coming. I had no control over the situation. I didn't know if this meant we would be getting back together or if this visit would really end it between us for good. I did know that I wasn't returning to New Jersey—that much was certain.

I glanced at the clock and saw that his plane arrived about an hour ago, which meant he would be here shortly.

Kavan was away again. *That boy is never home.* I think this trip was planned the second I told him Jaye was coming.

I was engrossed in my writing when I heard a car pull into the driveway. Jumping up, I dropped my pad and ran to the door. I planned on playing it cool, but that wasn't working. I couldn't get to the door fast enough. I swung it open, and there stood Jaye, looking finer than ever. I actually wanted to cry—that's how emotional I was. I almost said, "Freak it, I'm coming home," but I knew better.

Jaye dropped his bags and reached out to hug me with an unsure look on his face, and I fell into his arms.

"I missed you," he said.

"I missed you too." I didn't want to let him go. Breaking away, I said, "Maybe we should go in the house."

Like everyone did when they first walked in Kavan's house, he looked around and said, "I'm impressed. Homeboy is doing good, I see."

"That he is. That he is."

Jaye followed me into the living room, and we sat on opposite sides of the couch, neither saying a word. We were taking each other in. He still looked good. Not that I expected him to change that much in a few months.

Breaking the silence, Jaye said, "So, I'm finally here."

"That you are. How did you like the drive?"

"It was scenic."

Yep, we were making small talk when all I wanted to do was make love and all I wanted to know is what made him decide to visit. "Jaye . . . ?"

"Yes."

"Why are you here?"

"What do you mean?—a brother can't just come out to see you?"

"Of course, you can. I'm just curious. I was wondering why, after all these months, you decide to pop up."

He moved closer to me and took my hand. "I didn't call you on purpose. When you left I was angry and hurt. I felt like my most prized possession was stolen from me. Then I realized *that* was the problem—I treated you like an object and not a person. I knew to hear your voice would be unbearable. I wanted to call you and beg you to come home, but then I thought better of it. I decided to give you space. Then I didn't hear from you and decided to make a step and come out here."

"We both were wrong. We've been friends, lovers, mates for too long to let anger, resentment, and hurt come between us. I'm glad you're here, and I want to make the most of your trip." I was feeling proud of the way I was handling this.

"I want to make the most of it too." Looking around, he asked me for a tour.

I wanted to give him a tour straight to my bedroom, but decided not to rush the sex thing because it was bound to happen.

> *You're here*
> *I'm pleased*
> *I really dig your company*
> *Ms. Badu couldn't have said it any better*
> *My emotions to the letter*
> *You're at my door*
> *Back in my life*
> *Once my every thing*
> *Now my*
> *Unknown*

THAT NIGHT

We were lying in the bed, facing one another with our clothes on. I knew he wanted me just as much as I wanted him, but both of us were too afraid to make the first move. I couldn't help wondering if he would know that I'd been with another man. I also wondered if he'd been with anyone, especially that Lynn girl.

We didn't leave the house at all. We just sat and watched movies and caught up on one another.

It was almost ten o'clock when Jaye told me that he wanted to lie down.

"How about I lay with you?"

"I'd like that," he replied. "You're so beautiful." He ran one of his hands through my hair and stopped at the nape of my neck, pulling me closer to him.

I kissed him on the lips—okay, I tongued his ass down. Do you hear me?

"You want to take a shower together?" he asked.

"Yes."

We climbed out of the bed, and I led him to the bathroom. He didn't know that the bathroom also had a Jacuzzi in it; I figured I'd let that be a surprise. When he saw it, he said, "Shower's out, Jacuzzi's in."

I just smiled as I started to undress. I knew he was watching my every move, so I took my sweet-ass time, moving each piece of clothing seductively. Under my skirt I wore my sexy string thongs. I knew they would turn him on. I turned around and took my skirt off, making sure he saw every curve in my ass. When I was done, I climbed in. "Your turn."

He pulled his T-shirt over his head. His chest was tight, his abs were tight. He just looked delicious.

I felt my pussy walls tingle. *Damn, his body is chiseled.*

He pulled his sweats down. I loved to see him in those boxer briefs. The imprint of his dick made me want to reach out and grab it. He climbed in beside me, and the kiss started back where it left off, full of passion. There was none of that "a peck here, a peck there"; we'd both waited too long for this moment.

"Jaye, I need you inside me."

"How about I taste you first?"

"No, I need you inside me now." I straddled him and eased down on his dick, right there in the Jacuzzi. "God, I've missed you."

"I missed you too." He moved my hips up and down, as I ignored the ringing phone.

> *Taste me*
> *Feel me*
> *Explore every inch*

WESLEY

O kay, she got me with that one. I wasn't expecting her to say a guy was visiting. *Why didn't she tell me this shit sooner?* Mind games—homegirl was playing mind games. I wasn't one to be trifled with. *Maybe I'm going off a little too much. I don't know what's come over me.* I didn't want to scare her away; I wanted to bring her closer.

I planned on letting the phone ring until she picked up. I knew she was home. And if she wasn't, why didn't she pick up her cell phone when I called that? *I know her; either way, she'll answer one of them, especially when she doesn't know who is calling.* That's why I blocked my number out.

She had to be fucking whoever this friend is—that's the only reason a female won't answer her phone. *I'll get Quassmirah to call her.*

I couldn't do that. Couldn't let a sister know a brother was being played. I needed to calm my ass down—that's what I needed to do. We hadn't made anything official. We had a friendship and now a business relationship. Plus, I was jumping to conclusions; she said "a friend." They might be out having a good time. If he was only a friend, how come she didn't suggest I come by to meet him? Hell, she let me meet Keke.

You're probably going, *Why is he bugging?—he let her friend suck his dick.* I knew I was wrong and wasn't going to let it happen again.

Hell, I was a man who just got caught up out there, that was all. Besides, it was in Quassmirah's best interest not to say anything—especially if she wanted to make an album.

I decided to call Layla later, because I didn't want to be stressing over this shit. *Maybe she'll come to the gym in the morning.*

Sprung, you think
Nah, not that
I deny it
Knowing it's true
I'm hooked
Girl
On none other
Than you

GIRL, I'M LEAVING YOU AGAIN

The visit that started off like a honeymoon ended like a divorce—a nasty one. His first couple of days here were lovey-dovey. We couldn't keep our hands or mouths off each other. Once the lovemaking entered the picture, everything was forgiven and forgotten. I wasn't answering my phone, and I didn't go to the gym.

Wesley was calling, and so was Quassmirah. I wasn't thinking about them. My mind, my heart, and my body were all on Jaye. After the fifth day, the gym called me to teach a class because one of the instructors had an emergency. They all but begged.

"Do you want to come?"

"Nah, you go ahead."

I breathed a sigh of relief when Jaye said no. Don't ask me what I was thinking. I knew there would've been a chance of running into Wesley, but so what? I was a grown-ass woman, and he was a grown-ass man. Now the only thing I had to worry about was if Wesley was going to be at the gym.

When I entered the gym, I went straight to the aerobic room. (Even if Wesley was there, he'd be lifting weights; and the aerobic room and the weight room were in opposite directions.)

While teaching the class, I found myself looking towards the door every few seconds. I had the headphones and mic on. Which meant my voice would carry. So if he was there, he was sure to hear me.

When class was over, some of the women came up to me, trying to start a conversation. I told them I was in a hurry and would speak with them the next time I taught. I just needed to get out of there before Wesley saw me. I ran up the stairs and walked as fast as I could to the parking lot. As I was getting in my car, Wesley pulled up and he looked right at me.

Damn, damn, damn. There was no way I could just pull off, so I sat still while he approached the car.

"I've been trying to call you."

"I've been busy; I told you I was having a visitor."

He was quiet for a second or two. "Is this person your man from Jersey?"

"He's my ex-man."

"Your 'ex-man'?"

"Yes."

"And he came all this way to see you?"

"Yes."

"Are you getting back with him?"

"Not that it's any of your business—but no." I didn't appreciate the questions and thought he needed to take it down a notch.

"Listen, I'm sorry if it sounds like I'm being an asshole. It's just that I wanted to see you. I also needed to know if you put together that package for the video."

"I accept your apology. I was going to send the package to you this week."

He looked like he had something else on his mind. "Call me when your company leaves."

"I will." I watched him walk into the gym and pulled off. I thought everything was cool, but I was wrong.

A couple of days later Wesley called my house and Jaye answered the phone, since I was out running an errand.

WESLEY

When I saw Layla in the parking lot, I was glad and pissed at the same time. I knew something was up with this visitor, at least more than she was revealing. She had that "busted" look on her face.

Plus, I knew no brother was going to come across the country to see "a friend." I guarantee, he was here to get her back. I saw that if I wanted her, I was going to have to be more aggressive.

It had been a couple of days and I hadn't heard from Layla. She sent the final draft of the video via courier, with a note saying, she'll call me in a couple of days. Now what the hell was that about? I didn't want to wait a couple of days, so I picked up the phone to call her.

"Hello." A man answered the phone. I knew it wasn't Kavan; I knew his voice.

"Hello, I'd like to speak with Layla."

There was a slight hesitation on the phone. "May I ask, who's calling?"

I decided to be ignorant and see how far I could go with this. "A close friend of hers."

"Your name?"

"Wesley."

"And you say you're a close friend?"

"Yes."

"Do you mind if I ask how close?"

When he asked that, I knew that the shit was going to hit the fan. He sounded angry and suspicious. Now I could be a man about this and hang up the phone or I could be an ass-hole about it and taunt this fellow—that was my dilemma. Well, you know what . . . I chose to be an asshole, and as I was about to exaggerate about my relationship with Layla, Czar walked in. I couldn't have my boy see me go out like a sucker, so I said, "Just tell her I called. She has the number."

Busted and disgusted
What more can I say?
Yes, there was another way
To handle it
But I chose not to
Had to put my mack down
Who am I fooling
Other than myself
Look within
Not around

GOODBYES ARE
NEVER EASY

When I arrived home, Jaye was sitting on the couch. I walked over to give him a kiss.

We'd planned on going out that night to have dinner, perhaps go dancing, and then come back to the house to make love once again. It was like we couldn't get enough of each other.

We had yet to discuss us. Maybe we were procrastinating because he had an open ticket. But Kavan was coming home the next day, so this was going to be our last day of privacy.

I should have known something was wrong—Jaye was sitting on the couch without the TV or radio on.

When I went to kiss him, he turned his head. I asked him, "What is that about?"

"Who is Wesley?"

My eyes scanned the room, looking everywhere but at him. *What the hell . . . why was he asking me about Wesley? How would he even know Wesley's name?* I tried to think if I'd left anything lying around that would point in that direction, but I knew there was nothing. I decided to limit what I told him. "He's someone I'm doing business with."

"Really?"

"Yes. Really. You know that video I'm working on? Well, he's the producer and owner of the record label."

"Well, if it's business, how come he called here sounding all personal and shit, like it was more than business? Talking 'bout 'Tell her Wesley called' and 'I'm a close friend of hers.' "

"He said that?" I couldn't believe Wesley, a grown-ass man, would pull something like that, especially after I told him Jaye was my ex-man.

"Yes, he did. What does he mean by a close friend? I thought you told me you weren't seeing anyone."

I really didn't feel like getting all into it over Wesley. "I'm not."

Jaye would be leaving in a couple of days, and here we were arguing over a damn phone call. *Wait a minute—that means his ass answered my phone.* I wanted to ask him, "What gave you the right to answer my phone?" but I knew that would've started another argument. One of those "you-must-have-something-to-hide" arguments.

He patted the space next to him, and I sat down.

"Listen, please come home with me. I want to be with you; I want to get married; I want you to have my kids. I know it might seem like I had you on hold all these years—and I regret doing that—but I'm ready now. Ready for whatever you're ready for."

Shit, Kavan was right. He said Jaye was going to come and pull this "come-with-me, let's-get-married" stuff. He sounded so sincere, I wanted to hug him and say, "Yes, yes, I'll come and be with you." I knew that would be the wrong move because I would once again be giving up myself and my dreams.

"I don't want to come back to Jersey just yet. How come you can't come here and open a business here?" Even as I said it, I knew it wasn't that simple.

"Because my life is in Jersey."

"Well, my life is here now."

"And that's *with* or *without* me?"

It was a question that I didn't want to answer. "How come we can't have a long-distance relationship?"

"You know that's not going to work."

"It can, if we want it to."

"Well, it's not what I want—I want to be able to see you every day, not every now and then."

"Well, you should have thought about that a long time ago," I told him, full of spite, because it was obvious he was saying that it had to be his way or no way.

"You're going back to that, huh? I thought you understood the time, the money, none of it was right."

"I loved you—that's all that should have mattered . . . not how much money we had, not when the fucking time was right—love should have been enough." I thought about that line Halle Berry used in *Boomerang*—"Love should have brought your ass home last night."

I think we both knew in our heart of hearts that our relationship had run its course; that it was time for it to come to an end.

"I think I should leave today." He reached over towards me and pulled me in his arms, and I leaned against him. "I'll always love you," he told me.

"And I, you."

We both had tears in our eyes as he called the airport to find out flight times.

A couple of hours later when he walked out the door, I felt like my life had come to an end. I went into the bathroom and pulled out my Kama Sutra Bath and Body Oil and Candle, ran me some bath water, lit the candles, put on Phyllis Hyman, and fell apart.

I really thought Jaye and I would've come to some sort of understanding. Boy, was I wrong. He didn't even want me to

take him to the airport. After I thought about it, I should have
insisted and done it anyway. But no, my pride didn't allow it.

A part of my past
A significant part
Gone
Me
Alone
No one to comfort me
To hold me
To tell me
It'll be okay
It will
I'll hold on

KAVAN

When I arrived home the next day, I was surprised to find Layla sitting on the couch in the living room, alone, looking depressed. I knew immediately what happened. *That damn Jaye came here and broke her heart.* I turned the light on, kneeled beside her, took her hand, and looked in her eyes. "What's wrong, boo? It looks like you've been crying. Where's Jaye? Did he do something to you? Did he say something to you? Am I going to have to kick his ass?"

Knowing I was a lover and not a fighter, this caused her to smile just a little. "He's not here; he left. Went back to Jersey."

"I thought he was staying for a while."

"*Was* is the operative word," Layla said, her voice cracking.

I got up off my knees and rubbed them. "Being chivalrous is no joke—my damn knees hurt."

Layla smiled half-heartedly.

I sat next to her. "So what happened, honey?"

"We had an argument."

I wanted more information, but it was obvious Layla wasn't offering any. I wasn't sure whether to let it go or dig. The caring, nosy friend that I was, I chose to dig. "Well, that's a lot of information."

Layla laughed. "That's because I don't feel like getting into it. The disagreement was about the same old, same old—us being apart—him not wanting me out here, and me not wanting to go back to Jersey. It was a dead-end conversation that got heated and ended with him walking out. And the fact that he answered the phone when Wesley called and said he was a close friend of mine didn't help."

Before I could tell her what an asshole Jaye was, the phone rang.

Layla jumped up. "I'll get it." She snatched the phone off the receiver. "Hello." Disappointment was written all over her face when she said, "Hello, Quassmirah."

I frowned when I heard her name. TC called me while I was out of town and told me what he'd overheard in Wesley's office. I was going to tell her about it, but decided to wait a few days—she didn't need bad news on top of bad news.

Silence
Best kept
In times of despair
No need to hear
Or be the bearer
Of bad news
Causing the blues
Keep it to yourself
Sometimes
The time is never right

LIFE GOES ON AS USUAL

The first few days after Jaye left were hard. I planned on calling him the next afternoon but wanted to wait and see if he'd call me. He didn't.

I actually entertained the thought a time or two about going back to Jersey, but changed my mind when Wesley called and informed me that they were going to start shooting the video in two days and to come out. When I arrived and saw my words and thoughts being filmed, I knew I was in the right place—Los Angeles.

Just because I mentioned Wesley didn't mean I let him get away with not leaving a simple message when Jaye was here. We had a little confrontation. He said he didn't mean anything by it. I knew he was lying. That was the moment I made my decision not to be bothered with anything other than a business relationship with him—I couldn't stand liars and connivers. Besides, it was obvious that he wanted more from me than I wanted to give.

So instead of focusing on my personal life, I decided to focus on my professional life. I'd finally finished the final draft of one of my screenplays and was ready to submit it to agents and production companies. I also attended a film convention, where I made a few contacts and handed my script out. *You never know, someone just might show some interest.* I was anxious, knowing things didn't generally happen overnight, but I wished that maybe once, for me, they would.

Please come my way
Luck
Success
Love
I've waited long enough

SOMETHING'S NOT RIGHT

I woke up with a headache and an upset stomach. Something wasn't right—I had a bad feeling and wish I knew what it was, and I just couldn't shake the feeling. I tried to lie back down, but that didn't help either. I kept tossing and turning. The clock read 4:30 a.m. I tried to pray myself back to sleep, but it wasn't happening. So I climbed out of bed, went into the bathroom to brush my teeth, wash my face, and, perhaps, make me a cup of tea.

Walking down the stairs, I tried to be as quiet as possible when the phone rang. *Who the hell could be calling so early in the morning?* Now I knew something wasn't right. That gut instinct that woke me was for a reason. "Please, God," I whispered, "let everything be okay." I ran back into my room and answered the phone. "Hello."

"Hey," Justice said.

"What's up? Is everything okay? Why are you calling so early?"

The hesitation in his voice is what gave it away.

Just then Kavan walked into my room, rubbing his eyes. "Hey, girl, is everything all right? Who the hell is that calling so early?" Kavan had just got back in town that night and was asleep when I arrived home. He'd left a note saying he wanted to talk to me in the morning about something.

Justice blurted out, "Ali was in a bad car accident. He's in the hospital."

"What do you mean a bad accident? How bad?"

Kavan sat next to me on the bed. "Who was in an accident? Who are you talking to? What happened?" He was working both of us into a frenzy.

I didn't answer him. I was waiting on Justice to tell me what the hell he was talking about.

"You need to come home; he's in a coma."

I grabbed my chest which had tightened up, and started hyperventilating. I lost all self-control.

Kavan snatched the phone out of my hand. "Who is this? What the hell is going on?"

Obviously Justice was telling Kavan what happened because he reached over and pushed my head between my legs and rubbed my back. "I'll have her on the first flight out this afternoon." He hung up the phone and held me.

"Why, Kavan? Why?"

"Everything happens for a reason, honey."

Now that was the kind of bullshit I hated, when people say something like that—'Everything happens for a reason.' "A reason? A reason? What's the reason behind all the tragedies in this world? What's the reason behind devastation? Behind you having HIV? Behind 9/11? Behind the DC sniper? What's the reason behind my baby brother being in a coma?—tell me that."

He didn't respond.

"You can't answer me, can you? You know why?—because there is no reason." I was yelling at the top of my lungs.

Kavan took it like a soldier. "You're upset, so I'll let you yell at me. It's okay."

"It's not okay, Kavan. It's not okay." I put my head on his shoulder and dissolved into tears.

"Go lay down. Let me call the airport and find out what time the flight leaves, then we'll pack you some things, call a car, and you'll be on way to be with your family."

"Okay." I was feeling drained.

Kavan left the room, and I stood up looking in the mirror at my bloodshot red-rimmed eyes.

If God has a plan for everyone, I wish he would let me in on his secret. I threw myself across the bed. Before dozing off, I said a prayer asking God, *Please let my brother pull through; he's too young and has so much to offer the world. Please, let this coma be a temporary thing. Please don't take his life, and watch over my mother and keep her strong until I get there.*

I even promised to start attending church, a place I had not set foot in since coming to L.A. I knew better; we were raised in church.

I REMEMBER MY PARENTS waking us up one at a time to shower and get dressed. It was a ritual that eventually we grew out of. When we were little, we enjoyed going because of Sunday school and kid's church. While the adults had church, we got to play games, read, and do puzzles, all the time learning about Christ. As we grew older, church didn't really hold our interest. Well . . . me and Justice's interest; Ali still enjoyed attending. Justice and I were like, "Something's wrong with him."

I couldn't wait until I got older to decide whether I wanted to go or not. A few times my mother would send us by ourselves, and we'd go for the first half-hour then sneak out. Me and Justice would have to force Ali to come with us.

Now here my brother was laying up in a hospital in a coma. *Where was his God when the accident happened? What is it that they say?—Why do bad things happen to good people?* I knew it wasn't right to blame Him, but it was hard not to.

When my dad died, I think we all rebelled against religion.

Even Ali. That was the one time he openly defied mom when it came to church.

Kavan woke me up around nine o'clock.

"No one called in the middle of night, did they? I just had a bad dream, right?" I asked him.

The look on his face answered my question. He held out his hand and assisted me out the bed. "Come on, sweetie, you'll need to take a shower and make sure I packed what you might want to take. Your plane leaves in three hours. I want you to eat something, and then we'll leave for the airport."

All I could say was, "All right."

I did what was requested of me, and we were on our way to the airport, with me not saying a word, and Kavan trying to reassure me that everything would be okay.

How could he say that? He didn't know what was going to happen. I knew he was just trying to make me feel better and I appreciated it. But the last thing I needed was false hope.

He waited with me until my plane was called, gave me a kiss on the cheek, and said, "Call me if you need anything."

"I will."

Damn! I was on my way back to Jersey, not for a family visit, but for a family tragedy.

I was sitting on the plane in first-class once again, but this time it was Kavan who hooked me up. He wanted to make sure this six-hour flight was as comfortable for me as possible.

My eyes were closed, so I barely noticed those around me. Then I felt someone tap me on the shoulder. I looked up and saw Czar. Surprised, I said, "Hey."

"So, you're on your way home?"

I just nodded.

"So am I—mind if I sit next to you?" He sat down in the empty seat next to me.

"No, I don't mind."

He looked towards me. I knew he was taking in my puffy eyes and the fact that I probably looked a mess. "Is everything okay?"

Out of nowhere I started crying.

The unknown awaits
Guessing
Life
Death
The Purpose
Questions
Concerns
Unsure
Fear

CZAR SPEAKS

I asked her if she was okay, and she broke down crying. I didn't have to do that when I could clearly see that she wasn't. I was one of those brothers who hated to see a sister cry. My sisters knew that if they wanted something from me, the way to get it was to cry. I had to learn to distinguish real tears from fake ones because I would end up buying clothes, diamonds, and cars.

The tears falling down Layla's cheeks were as real as a two-dollar bill. *Damn, she looked good*—tears and all. I thought so the first day I met her at the bar. I actually noticed her the second she walked in and was getting ready to approach her when I noticed she was with Wesley.

Now, Wesley was my boy and had been for quite some time. Since our early teens. We sold drugs together. He got out the game before me, and when I got shot, I knew it was time for me to get out as well. Not only was I putting my life in jeopardy, but those of my two sisters as well. Both parents dead from cancer—*now ain't that some shit*—my older sister, Kat, kept us together and did the best she could raising us. She was 19, Kymm was 15, and I was 12.

I was on my way home because she was just diagnosed with

cancer and called and said she wanted to see me, that she needed me. I loved my sisters. In fact, I spoiled them and enjoyed being able to do it. I felt like it was my turn to take care of them.

Now back to Layla—I was feeling her big time. Wesley was one lucky man. He just didn't know it. That day I walked in on him and Quassmirah, I felt like something was up. They both had this look on their face.

Of course I asked Wesley about it, and he was like, "Ain't nothing." Now we'd been "boys" for quite some time and I knew when he was lying. But I decided not to press it. He'd be a fool to mess up what he had or could've had with Layla, because a brother like me would be on it, wining and dining her, spoiling the shit out of her. Just from the few times I'd seen her and hung out with her, I'd say she was the kind of woman a brother would make his wife. So to see her sitting here crying her eyes out made me want to hold her. Made me want to assure her that everything was going to be all right, kiss her, and say, "I'll make it better; I'll be your hero."

> *I'm here to save you*
> *From destruction*
> *I want to carry you in my arms*
> *Away from the dangers*
> *That lurk in the corners*
> *I want to be your hero*
> *The one you turn to*
> *In fear*
> *The one you turn to*
> *With hope*
> *I'm here*
> *You're there*
> *Just ask*

TEARS

He asked me what was wrong with such concern and sensitivity, I found myself telling him what happened to Ali.

"That's unfortunate. I know how it feels to maybe lose a loved one."

"You do?"

"Yeah, I'm going to see my sister. She has cancer. She called and asked me to come home, so that can only mean bad news."

I felt for him but even more for myself. It was just that your stuff, your sorrow, it always seemed worse than the other person's. Not taking away from his pain, I just thought that with cancer you kind of knew the outcome, but with a car accident, you could be here today and gone tomorrow.

Looking up at him, I felt like an inconsiderate ass even thinking those thoughts because looking into his eyes made me realize that pain is pain.

"I love my brothers. We've always been tight and just to imagine, just to think, that the three of us may not be able to—"

Czar put his arms across my shoulders, and I put my head on his. We sat that way for over an hour, lost in our thoughts.

184 / *Angel M. Hunter*

Clearing his throat, Czar looked down at me and asked, "So are you and Wesley an item?"

"No, we're just working together. Why?"

"Just curious." After a slight hesitation, he added, "I was under the impression that it was more than a business relationship."

"Could have been, but not now." *Oops, I let that slip out.*

This caught Czar's attention. "Why not?"

Shit, I had already let the cat out the bag. Might as well let it all the way out. I liked Czar, and like I said before, I could see me and him being friends; I just wasn't too sure how that would work, with him being Wesley's boy.

"I just don't see me and him going anywhere, relationship-wise. I know that's what he wants, but my intuition is telling me it just won't work."

The flight attendant pranced down the aisle, eyeing Czar. I was surprised to find a little jealous tingle go through me. *What was that all about?* I looked at him to see if he noticed her.

He did, because he was smiling when she stopped and asked, "Is there anything I can do for you, sir?"

It was obvious that she meant *anything* too.

Laughing, Czar looked over at me and asked me if there was anything I needed.

"I'd like a glass of wine," I told him. "White wine."

Looking back at the airline stewardess, he told her, "And a shot of Scotch would be nice."

She gave him the biggest smile, not once looking at me. "I'd be right back."

I rolled my eyes and commented, "Well, that was interesting."

"What?"

"Do you think she even saw me?"

He just laughed.

The rest of the flight was smooth. We talked, laughed, and I cried some more. I was seriously feeling him. It was a shame

I couldn't do anything about it. *Why couldn't I have met him first?*

As arrival time approached, I looked over at Czar and took his hand. "Thanks for distracting me and making me feel better; I really appreciate it."

Gently pulling his hand away, he reached in his pocket and pulled out a card. Then he wrote a phone number on the back of it and told me, "If you need anything—and I stress *anything*—call me. I'm talking about a shoulder to cry on or just someone to listen. Pick up the phone; I'm only a hop, skip, and a jump away."

I took the card. "I'll keep that in mind." I gave him the number to my mother's and told him to give me a call, if he needed to talk as well. I leaned back in the seat and closed my eyes and asked God to give me the strength to face whatever it was I needed to.

Grant me the serenity
Dear Lord
To accept what I may not be able to change
Give me strength
Courage
Carry me
Through these troubled times
I need your help
Amen

DEATH OR LIFE

As soon as I stepped off the platform, with Czar walking beside me, I looked around and wondered who would be picking me up from the airport. I didn't have to wonder long.

"Layla! Layla!" It was Keke, headed in my direction. Her face full of questions, she looked at me then at Czar. Not one to hold her tongue, she said, "Well, well, well, what do we have here?"

Czar hugged her. "It's nice to see you again, Keke."

She returned his embrace, while looking at me.

I turned towards Czar. "I hope everything is okay with your sister. I'll call you."

He kissed me on the cheek. "Make sure you do that." Then to Keke, "You take good care of her."

Keke saluted. "Yes, sir."

We watched him walk away.

"Isn't he something?" I said to Keke, staring as hard as I was.

"That he is. That he is."

We went to get my bags. Neither of us said a word until we got in the car. Breaking the silence, I asked her about Ali. I knew she went to see him and had probably been with my family since the accident. (My mother saw her as a daughter.)

"I don't know what to tell you, sweetie. I don't want to upset you and I don't want to scare you. I know you know he's in a coma."

Hearing those words tore me up inside. "Do you think he's going to make it? Is he breathing on his own? Is he hooked up to machines?"

In the sweetest voice she could muster up, Keke said, "I don't know if he's going to make it or not."

"But you're a doctor."

"How about we wait until we get to the hospital?"

I was burnt out, full of fatigue and just plain old scared. We pulled into the parking lot of the hospital, and Keke parked the car. "Are you ready?" she asked.

Truthfully, I wasn't. I was afraid of what I might find when I walked in. I was scared shitless, let me tell you. With all these questions running through my mind, I knew I was working myself up to another anxiety attack. I put my hand up to my chest and told myself, "Breathe in, breathe out."

"Come on, sweetie, we have to go in. They're waiting on us." Seeing the panic in my face, Keke placed her hand over mine. "Relax. It's going to be okay. Say a quick prayer. Your mother, Justice, me—we're all here."

I removed my hand from underneath hers and asked God to give me the strength I would need to face whatever I was about to face. I tried to put on a brave face and summon up the courage to go inside.

"Are you okay?" Keke asked.

"I'm fine," I lied.

As I entered the hospital, I glanced around the waiting room. I hated hospitals, especially the stench. It was a sickening sweet smell of mildew and pine-sol. Walking past visitors, employees and patients, I couldn't help noticing that no one smiled. Everyone had this dead-ass, emotionless look on their faces.

I followed Keke to the elevator. Imagine my surprise to find

Jaye and the bitch, Lynn, in a nurse's uniform nonetheless, standing at the elevator when we finally reached the floor. *Please don't let her be one of my brother's nurses.* I walked right by them without acknowledgment.

Jaye moved away from her and said, "Layla, wait."

Keke stopped walking. I grabbed her arm and pulled her along. I didn't even bother to look behind me because I knew he was following us; I started moving even faster.

"Don't be like that," Keke said in a low tone; "he cares about your brother just as much as you do."

We reached my brother's room, and before stepping in, I once again asked the Lord to give me strength. The second I saw my brother laying on that hospital bed, tubes everywhere, looking lifeless, I broke down. I looked at him and tried to understand how one could go from being healthy, physically fit, strong; able to conquer to the world, to almost spiritless.

Someone pulled out a chair, and I collapsed into it sorrow-stricken. Jaye was standing on one side on me rubbing my shoulders as I sobbed, and Justice was kneeling in front of me, holding my hand. My mother was watching silently and moving her lips—I knew she was praying.

I shook Jaye's hand away and took mine from beneath Justice. "I'll be right back."

Jaye started to follow me, but I stopped him. "Stay here. I need to be alone." I went into the bathroom, threw water on my face, looked into the mirror and saw a lot of anger and hostility. It was eating me up and I knew it wasn't doing me any good.

Forgetting all about the prayers I'd said prior to arriving, I wondered how my mother could pray to a God that would allow her child to be on what may become his deathbed. How a God could allow something like this to happen to someone who'd never hurt anyone, someone as good and kind as my brother. I needed to understand this—there were so many evil-ass people in this world—killers, rapists, drug dealers, the list could go on—and don't shit happen to them. *Explain that to me.*

I was washing my hands, trying to cleanse my soul. Cleanse my thoughts. My mother walked in. We just looked at one another.

"Why, Mommy? Why?"

She held me in her arms. "It's going to be okay. It's going to be okay," she kept repeating. I wondered if she was trying to convince me or herself. "Come on, it's time to see your brother, talk to him, touch him. Don't be afraid. He's going to get through this."

When we walked back in the room, all eyes were on me. Everyone looked like they wanted to offer words of comfort. I let everyone know I was all right. I moved over to the bed where my brother lay naked, except for a towel. I smiled. He looked so beautiful and peaceful, like a Greek god. You could see his strength. "Ali, come on, you can get through this," I said out loud. "You can get through this. We're all here rooting for you."

I continued to talk to him, hoping he could hear what I was saying. I told him all about California and the video I worked on. I told him that I wanted him to come visit when he got better. I talked and talked until a nurse came in and asked everyone to leave so they could bathe him. Everyone left the room, except me and my mom.

"Don't you want to go grab something to eat?" my mother asked.

"No, I'm staying right here," I told her.

We moved to the side while the nurses bathed him. It hit me that I didn't know what happened, what caused the accident.

"What happened, Ma?"

"I'm not sure. All I know is that Tracy was driving and—"

"Tracy was driving? Where is she?"

"She's upstairs in another room."

"Upstairs in another room? Is she all right?"

"Yes. Shaken up and bruised, but other than that, fine."

"Whose fault was it?" None of that should have mattered, but I needed to know; I needed to place blame. All the while, I thought Ali was driving, and to hear that Tracy was threw me for a loop.

The second she hesitated, I knew. I knew that hoochie was at fault. "I'll be back." I wanted to go upstairs and bust her in her head.

"Layla, please wait. Think about whatever it is you're about to do; everyone is in pain here, not just you."

I didn't say a word. I just looked at her and wondered how she knew I was about to go upstairs and start some drama. *How could she be fine with a few bumps and bruises and my brother is laying here with us not knowing if he's going to make it or not?*

"I don't understand, Ma—how is she fine and Ali not? What did she do?"

"All I know, right now, is she was going through a yellow light and someone ran into them."

"What about the seatbelt? Ali always wears his seatbelt. What about the airbags?—they're supposed to save you."

"Come on, let's go in the hall." My mother glanced over at the nurses.

"Why are you looking at them? I don't care about them, I care about my brother. I care about what happened." I was once again hysterical, and Keke and everyone were coming towards us.

My mother threw up her hands to stop them. She put her hands under my chin. "You listen, girlie, don't you go upstairs starting no shit, you hear me? It was an accident. Think about how many times you've ran a yellow light; we've all done it."

"Yeah, we have, but I never just about killed anyone either."

"This is not the time to show your behind. That girl feels guilty enough as it is. Let her work through it. What we need to use our energy for is prayer and faith, you hear me? Prayer and faith. Your brother will pull through this. We just have to believe, we have to be here for him, we have to talk to him, we have to touch him; he needs to feel our presence. God is amazing, Layla—He can do all things."

Instead of going upstairs and cursing Tracy out, instead of beating her down for destroying my brother, I decided to listen to my mother and use my energy for something more useful and productive. This faith and prayer thing, I was going to work on. I knew I needed to draw my strength from somewhere. *Maybe, just maybe, God would end up being the answer.*

"I know you're probably blaming God, but everything happens for—"

I didn't even let her finish. That was the last thing I wanted to hear, so I walked away, right by Keke, Justice, Jaye, and Lynn, the nurse.

Justice came behind me. "Don't do this, Layla."

Stopping, I faced him. "Do what?"

"Shut everyone out—I won't allow it."

"You won't allow it? Who are you to allow anything?" I lashed out.

"Listen, I know you're speaking from emotion, so I'm going to ignore what you just said. We need to be strong for one another; we need to be there for each other. This is not the time to be distant. Like mommy said, we need to have positive energy around Ali."

"Okay, okay, I get it. Damn." I looked down the hall at everyone staring at us. I looked over at Jaye and Lynn. "So are they dating each other?"

"I don't know."

I knew he was lying. I also knew I would find out sooner

than later, because in this small-ass town, any and everything was bound to come out.

I'm losing it
I know it and can't help it
I need to have control
To keep it on lock
Not to explode
Boom
There I go
Where or how far
Only God knows

I DON'T KNOW WHAT TO DO

I stayed the night at the hospital every day for a week, reading and talking to Ali. I couldn't bring myself to leave; my being there made me feel like I was his tower of strength. My mother stayed as well. I'd decided if it was going to take our voices to bring him out of this, I would talk myself tired. If it was going to take touch, I would bathe him, brush his hair, and kiss his face. I wanted so badly for him to just wake up, to move, to make a sound, but it just wasn't happening.

"Come on, you can get through this, you can do this. Wake up, Ali. We all love you. You're still young. You've got so many things to do, so many places to see. We've got to go on vacation. Please wake up." This went on all night.

At some point my mother convinced me to go downstairs to the cathedral.

What the heck! What would it hurt?

We prayed for what seemed like hours, and I felt a peace that surpassed all understanding.

When the morning came, my mother told me to go on home and get cleaned up.

"Okay, but I'll be back."

She smiled. "I know you will."

When I got to the house, Justice was at the kitchen table. "How's mom?" he asked.

"Stronger than I would be."

He nodded.

My mother was holding down the fort. *You never know a person's strength until something tragic happens.* I thought my mother was Superwoman, the Bionic Woman, and Jesus combined.

"How does she do it?"

We looked at each other.

"Prayer and faith," I told him, "her answer for everything. I'm going to take a shower, change, and head back to the hospital."

As I was walking off, Justice said, "Some guy named Czar called. Said give him a call when you get a free moment. Kavan called also."

I smiled and headed towards that shower.

I decided to call Kavan.

"Are you okay? How's the family? Do you want me to come out there?"

"No, Kavan, you don't have to do that. We're hanging in there, hoping for the best."

"Wesley's been calling here, and that hoochie, wannabe-singer friend of yours called too. I told them you were out of town."

"Thanks. You know I don't know when I'll be back."

"I know."

We were making small talk when Justice yelled upstairs that Jaye was here.

"I'll call you later this afternoon," I told Kavan. "I love you."

"I love you too."

We hung up, and I went downstairs to talk to Jaye, taking my slow-ass time, mind you. Yes, I was a little upset about seeing him talking to that wench Lynn—a lot upset and a lot jealous. Then to top everything, to make my day, she was one of my brother's nurses. I'd looked at the pad at the foot of his bed and saw that she'd signed off on a lot of treatments. *Ain't that some shit.* I just hoped I didn't have to beat her ass, because with all the tension and all the pent-up frustration, I was ready to let someone catch it.

When I entered the room, Jaye was sitting on the couch, flicking the remote control, looking burdened. I stood there for a second or two watching him, trying to figure out how to exist around him.

"How are you holding up?" were his first words.

Me and my simple, sensitive ass busted out in tears. And I'm not talking about "they-fell-silently-down-my-cheeks" type but the "cry-me-a-river" kind. They came out of nowhere.

Jaye wrapped his arms around me and pulled me into him. Wait, I might have collapsed into them. Although my mind and stubbornness told me to pull away, my heart and the need for comfort didn't allow it. So I cried myself dry, while he rubbed my back. I let go of everything I'd been holding in since the flight and especially since seeing my brother.

Finally I pulled away and took a long look at him. *Damn him.* I still loved him. I had to be honest with myself—we were on opposite sides of the coin and I just wasn't willing to sacrifice my life once again just to please another. Hell, I was the product of my brainstorm, and if I put my life on hold, it would've been no one's fault but my own.

"I still can't believe this is happening," he said.

"I know," I told him; "I wish I could understand it."

"None of us do."

We grew quiet.

Jaye broke the silence. "I miss you."

I threw my hands up. "Please don't go there."

"I have to, Layla, I regret walking out on you in Cali; I let my macho pride get the best of me."

He really wasn't saying much of anything, at least nothing I wanted to hear. He wasn't saying he'll come to L.A. and be with me, he wasn't saying maybe this can work, so before he went any further, I cut him off. "So what's up with you and Lynn?"

"Me—me and Lynn?"

Yep, caught him off guard.

"We're just friends."

"Jaye, you don't have to lie to me. I'm not stupid you know. I saw you and her talking, and there was definitely intimacy there."

"I'm not lying—we're just friends. We went out a couple of times, but that's what friends do."

I rolled my eyes. I couldn't believe he was trying to run that "she's-just-a-friend-we-only-went-out-a-couple-of-times" line. "Jaye, you don't have to explain anything to me; you're free to do what you want to do—I have no ties on you anymore." As I said those words, I felt a slight release. I was letting go of a long-time love, and it hurt like hell.

Jaye looked at me with misty eyes. For a second there, I thought he was about to break down.

Sparing him, I stood up and said, "Look, I have to get back to the hospital."

"Want me to go with you?"

"No, I'll probably stay the night there."

"How about I come keep you company then?"

I wanted to say yes, but I told him, "How about I call you?"

"Are you putting me out?" he asked with a confused look.

"No, I'm not," I lied. "We mean too much to each other for me to put you out; I just have some things I need to do before I return to the hospital."

He leaned forward to kiss me, and you know what, I let him—full on the mouth, tongue and all. I knew it would be the last time.

The last time
We kissed

I cried
Inside
I died
I fell apart
Gone with you
My heart
The last time
We kissed

WHAT DOES IT MEAN?

It had been two weeks and I was still in Jersey. There really hadn't been any change with my brother, and Jaye and I had been kicking it occasionally. We'd established a new friendship, and it felt weird. Of course, he tried on more than one occasion to get the coochie. And of course I wanted to say yes, but a sister was strong.

I was on the phone calling Wesley, when the doorbell rang. Kavan told me Wesley had called numerous times, sounding all concerned, and wanted the number to where I was, but of course, Kavan wouldn't give it to him.

He picked up as I opened the door to find a flower delivery. "Hello."

"Hi, Wesley." I took the card from the delivery guy.

"Layla, I've missed you. I've been trying to call you."

I read the card: *Thinking of you, call me when you have a moment. A friend, Czar.* I smiled and read the card again. I took the flowers, carried them in the house, and put them on the table.

"I know. Kavan gave me the messages. I've just been so busy going back and forth from the hospital, I haven't had time for anything or anyone."

"How's your brother?"

"The same. There hasn't been any change."

"I'm sorry to hear that. Do you need anything? Want me to come out there?"

"No, that's okay—I don't need anything other than your prayers." I wanted to get off the phone so I could call Czar and thank him for the flowers.

"Do you know when you'll be returning?"

"I don't know. I'm just taking it one day at a time. I'll stay here for as long as I have to." Actually, I hadn't given it any thought; that was the last thing on my mind. And I couldn't believe he would even ask me that. I didn't know the final outcome of my brother's condition and he wanted to know when I'd be coming back. *I thought that was some inconsiderate shit.*

He pushed the issue. "I'd love to come see you."

"I wouldn't be able to give you any time."

"That's okay."

"No, it's not okay. Listen, Wesley, what you want and what I want don't coincide—we're friends and that's it." I glanced at the flowers again. "I have to go."

"All right, but don't wait so long to call me; I miss hearing from you."

Didn't he hear one word I said? "Bye."

I called Czar.

We'd been speaking at least every other day over the past two weeks—he was still in New York—and I was enjoying every second of it. Whenever we talked I felt like a schoolgirl with a crush. His sister wasn't doing well either, and we sort of bonded over our sorrow.

"Hey, thanks for the flowers. They're beautiful."

"For a beautiful lady."

Not one to beat around the bush, I said, "How about coming to visit me?"

"I'd like that—when?"

"Today."

CZAR

Damn, she told me to come over today. Not tomorrow; not next week—today. Can you tell a brother was happy as hell? I couldn't get this girl out of my mind. I was seriously feeling her and trying not to press up too hard too quick. One reason being, she was vulnerable right now, and I didn't want to violate that. And the other is my boy Wesley. I knew I was messed up for pursuing this at all.

We'd connected on a level that I'd never been on with another female. It was hard to explain. You know how people talk about love at first sight—I was starting to believe it. She even sent my sister a cross and a card with a poem about hope. Can you believe that? I was blown away.

I wasn't going to let this girl get away. I had these feelings for her and I think she felt the same way. Eventually we're going to have to let Wesley know, and the shit will hit the fan for sure. This was going to have to be handled with kid gloves; that much I knew.

Matters of the heart pull you one way
Sometimes the wrong turn

Can lead you to the right person
Leaving joy
In a once empty place
Matters of the heart
You can't hide

OUR TIME TOGETHER

I asked Czar if he wanted to stop by the hospital with me. "Are you sure?"

"Of course, I'm sure."

So off to the hospital we went. When we arrived, Jaye was leaving and heading towards the parking lot. I stalled, applying lipstick on so we wouldn't run into one another.

When we reached the room I asked him if he wanted to come in and meet my mother and brother.

"I'd be honored."

We walked in the room and saw my mother sitting on the bed, holding Ali's hand and praying. We stood silently by the side until she was done. She must have felt our presence because she opened her eyes and waved us over. We walked over to the foot of the bed.

"Ma, this is Czar. Czar, this is my mother and my brother."

I'd told my mother about his situation. She stood up and gave him a big hug. "I'm praying for your sister."

"Thanks, I'm praying for Ali as well."

I asked my mother, "Is Ali showing any improvement?"

"You were here a few hours ago, sweetie, not much has changed."

"Well, you keep saying, 'Expect a miracle'—and don't forget about my dream."

The night before, I dreamed that Ali came out of the coma.

We were all standing over him praying when he opened his eyes and asked, "Why are you all standing over me?" The dream was clear as day and it felt so real. I woke up expecting Ali to be out of the coma, but it wasn't the case.

Czar and I kept my mother company for an hour, then we left to have dinner. Later that night, we were sitting in his car saying our goodbyes. I didn't want him to leave. As if reading my mind, he said, "I don't want to go."

"I don't want you to," I told him.

"Well, what are we going to do about it?"

I wanted to say he could stay at my mom's house, but that would've been disrespectful. So I suggested, "Um, would you mind getting a room?"—I was embarrassed and anxious asking him that—"I'll stay with you."

"You don't have to. I'll get a room either way . . . especially if it means spending more time with you."

"I know I don't have to. I want to." *What a gentleman!* Here I was putting the ass, literally, on the line, and he was saying that's not all he wanted.

Starting up the car, he said, "Lead the way."

"Let me run in the house and put together a bag." I also wanted to call the hospital and let Ma know that I'd be out and she could catch me on the cell phone.

When we pulled up to the Sheraton, I felt like a kid about to get busted doing something she had no business doing. I was actually excited and horny.

He reached over the backseat and grabbed my bag.

I didn't wait for him to open my door. I got out the car and waited for him to walk around so we could walk up to the hotel together. I glanced around to see if anyone I knew was in the area. There wasn't. Not that I would have cared—I was a grown-ass woman, after all—but this "going to a hotel with a man" was a new thing to me.

Czar went to the front desk and paid for our room.

Weary and fatigued, I followed him to the elevator. We'd spent all day together, not tiring of each other. I was ready for a good night's rest, *but then again a good night's sex would be even better.*

He turned the key and we entered the room.

I put my bag down and sat on the bed; he put his down and sat next to me. I glanced around and was pleased with what I saw. I was glad we hadn't chosen just any hotel because it would have taken away from the ambiance.

"So?" he said.

"So?"

"Do you want to watch TV?"

"Maybe. But there's something I would like even more."

"What's that?"

"A kiss."

When our lips met, I could have sworn I saw fireworks—his lips were so soft—and when his tongue found mine, I melted. I wrapped my arms around his neck and pushed him back on the bed.

"I like you being aggressive."

Normally, I wasn't this aggressive, but it felt right. I was laying on him and could feel the pressure of his penis on my hip. I looked up at him and smiled.

"You're so damn sexy—do you know that?"

I didn't answer him.

"What do you want to do? We'll only go as far as you want it to."

I answered by kissing him on his eyes, his nose, his cheeks, and finally his lips. I looked him in the eyes. "I want you; you want me. What we're getting into?—I don't know. But let's just take this moment for what it is; let's not think too much on it, let's not analyze it, let's just be—can we do that?"

He smiled. "We can do that."

"Good." I climbed off him and suggested we shower. "I feel gritty."

"Together?"

"Yes, together." I laughed and walked away to start the shower. I couldn't help wondering what had gotten into me. Normally I wasn't this bold. Well, actually, I'd never had the chance to be this bold, and it felt kind of good.

Yes, Czar and I managed to avoid the topic of Wesley, but I knew once we consummated our relationship, it would come up for discussion.

We were in the bathroom and I had just turned the water on when I heard my cell phone ringing. It was late as hell, and no one called me this late. So I knew it was an emergency. Running into the room and grabbing my phone out of the bag, I looked at the caller ID and saw it was the hospital.

Czar looked at me. "Is everything okay?"

"It's the hospital," I told him, fearing the worst.

"Answer it."

I pressed the talk button. "Hello?"

"Layla, Layla." It was my mother. She was crying. The sound of her weeping made me start to cry.

Czar moved closer to me and wrapped his arms around me.

"Come to the hospital."

"What happened? What's wrong with Ali?" I brought my hand up to my chest.

"Nothing's wrong, honey; everything is right—he woke up."

I dropped the phone in disbelief.

Czar picked it up and handed it back to me.

"He woke up. He woke up." I couldn't stop repeating it.

Czar went into the bathroom and turned the water off.

"I'm on my way."

"I'll wait here for you," Czar said.

I knew he was trying to be respectful and he probably felt like my family would want to be alone with Ali, but I wanted him there. If not in the room, at least somewhere close by.

"No. Come with me, please."

I didn't have to ask twice.

In the car, I called Keke and told her the good news.

"I'll meet you at the hospital," Keke said.

After I hung up with her, I leaned back, closed my eyes, and said a silent prayer, thanking God for that miracle. You have no idea how many times I'd all but given up. How many times I wondered if we were praying in vain. If it was all for nothing. I'd fussed, cussed and argued with God at least once daily, yet He still saw it fit to heal Ali.

"Can't you go a little faster?" I asked Czar.

I wanted to hold my brother, kiss him, tell him how much I love him and let him know how much he meant to me. I swore that we get would get even closer from that day forth.

"I'm going as fast as I can; we'll get there, don't worry."

Twenty minutes later I walked in my brother's room. My mother and Justice were there. They were standing in front of the bed, blocking my view. Czar was waiting down the hall, giving us our time yet being my support.

As I got closer to the bed, Ali looked up at me with a twinkle in his eye and a lopsided grin. Unable to contain myself, I ran over to him and wrapped my arms around him, put my head on his chest and cried.

Justice and Keke were crying with me. My mother, probably all cried out, was smiling from ear to ear, saying over and over, "Thank you, Jesus."

Lifting my head up, I took his hand in mine. "I can't believe this."

"Man, you just don't know—I was scared. I love you so much."

He tried to say something. I couldn't make out what it was.

I moved closer to his mouth. In a slow drawl, he was trying to say he loved me too. Let me tell you, hearing those words come from someone I thought wasn't going to live, took on a whole new meaning. Actually, being in the room with a real miracle gave life a whole new meaning.

I'm telling you; from this day forward things are going to change.

Life
So precious
A gift
Each day
Each moment
Each breath
To be shared
To be cherished
To be handled
With care

TWO WEEKS LATER

Czar's sister didn't make it. Cancer took her from him, and he was devastated. I felt for him; *almost* losing my brother was trying enough.

So much had happened these past two weeks. For one, Czar and I never made love, but we connected on a much deeper level. I knew that we were going to have to tell Wesley what was going on. We planned on continuing to see each other once we got back to California.

The reason I was going back was because Kavan called me with some news. "Girl, have I got some good news for you."

"It can't get any better than Ali coming out of his coma."

"I know that's right, but it's up there."

"Stop teasing me and get on with it."

"Well, you received a phone call from a producer."

My heart started racing. "I did? Who?"

"Bernard Irby."

"Get the hell out of here. You're lying."

"If I'm lying, I'm flying."

"Well, what did he say?"

"He wants to meet with you in regards to one of your scripts."

I couldn't believe it. Bernard Irby was one of the top producers at On Time Productions. They'd produced two of the top-grossing African American films over the past two years. Though neither one of them was a blockbuster hit, they didn't exactly lose money either. Seeing it was still considered a new company, if I got in, then who was to say what could happen?

Kavan gave me the number to Bernard's office. Right after our conversation ended I was calling the number.

"Bernard Irby's office, how may I help you?"

"Yes, this is Layla Simone. I'm returning Mr. Irby's call."

"Bernard Irby speaking."

I told him who I was.

"When can we meet?"

"Well, I'm in New Jersey right now, and the plan was to fly back to California in two days." I made it up as I went along.

"How about we meet Monday?"

That was five days away, more than enough time. "That would work."

I called Keke to share the news with her. You would have thought she was the one with the opportunity. She was screaming and yelling. "I'm on my way to the hospital," she told me, when she finished congratulating me.

Keke had been spending a lot of time at the hospital with Ali. I was getting suspicious, but in a good way. *That would be cool as hell—my brother and my best friend.*

His ex-girlfriend, Tracy, the cause of the accident, was so filled with guilt, she couldn't face the family. She was a coward, if you asked me. Had it been me that caused so much pain, I'd be kissing ass. The only thing that kept me from whupping her behind, was knowing that "what goes around, comes around" and that she'd probably be miserable until she at least apologized.

When I arrived at the hospital, Ali was just coming back from physical therapy. This was the hardest part—watching him re-learn how to walk, talk, and perform routine daily activities. It was heart-rending to see, but he was alive and that was what mattered, the most.

He was also taking it in stride; doing the best he could. Over and over he would say, the best way he knew how, "I can do all things through Christ, which strengthens me."

As it turned out, Lynn ended up being his primary nurse. Out of all the nurses in the hospital, it had to be the one I detested. I decided to be the bigger person; well, I decided to be civil and not hate on a sister. It was taking up way too much energy. Plus, she was taking good care of Ali.

Lynn and Jaye were dating one another. Whether it was exclusive or not, I didn't know.

One evening Czar and I were sitting on the porch when Jaye pulled up. Czar knew who he was from looking through my family's photo albums and seeing pictures of us together. I'd also told Czar who he was and how long we'd been together.

Czar asked, "Do you want me to go inside?"

"No."

Jaye parked his car and flipped. Homeboy went straight ignorant on a sister. "So who's your friend?" he asked, no beating around the bush, no hello, no nothing.

"Czar, this is Jaye. Jaye, this is Czar."

Looking at Czar, Jaye asked, "So are you two serious?"

Czar raised his eyebrow, looking a little too ready for battle. To keep the peace, I said to Jaye, "Let's go in the house."

"Why can't we talk out here?"

"Excuse us," I said to Czar. I grabbed Jaye by the hand and pulled him into the house. Once in the house, I asked Jaye, "What the hell is your problem?"

"Problem? Problem? I don't have a problem. I came by to see you, only to find some other nig—man on the porch all up in your face."

"What? I can't have company? We're not a couple any more, Jaye. You can't tell me who I can or can't see or what I can and can't do."

"I've never told you what you—" He stopped mid-sentence and took a deep breath. "Just forget it. Listen, I just wanted to stop by and chill with you. But I can see that you're occupied, so I'll just leave."

I didn't know what to say. Actually, there was nothing to say other than, "All right, we'll talk later." I should have told him to tell Lynn hello, but that would have been instigating for no apparent reason other than being bitchy.

It wasn't long afterwards when I saw Jaye and Lynn at the movies. Taking a break from the hospital, Keke and I decided to catch a flick. I could have kept walking, but decided to make sure they saw me. I sat right across from them. Keke said I was dead wrong. Maybe I was, but I didn't care.

The next day, Lynn approached me by saying, "Your brother is doing so well."

"Thanks."

"It's nice to see the family come so often. I think that's what pulled him through."

I didn't feel like small talk. We'd never had it before, and there was no reason to start now. "What do you want?"

"Straight to the point, huh?"

"Yes, straight to the point."

"Well, I just hope there are no hard feelings now that I'm dating Jaye."

I just looked at her and walked away. Keke was standing down the hall and witnessed our interaction.

"Don't you think you a bit rude towards her?" Keke asked when I reached her.

"I don't have shit to say to her. If it's not about my brother's treatment, what is there to talk about?"

"You're being such a bitch. What happened to your 'life-is-too-short-for-negative-energy' attitude?"

"I-I-I—" What could I say? She was right—I was being a bitch. I decided to put that attitude in check quickly; it wasn't healthy.

Attitudes
Are for the miserable
Attitudes
Are for those who have only themselves
For the sorry and the weak
Get it together
Reach out
Don't be so angry
Know
You are not alone

BACK IN CALI

Back in California the first thing I decided to do once I got comfortable was go to the gym. I needed to sweat; to work off all the emotions that had built up inside my body like toxin.

I hadn't really spoken to Wesley in a couple of weeks, and it wasn't because he didn't try to call me. I was avoiding him. I knew I could no longer handle this situation that way because we were bound to run into one another. Plus, I wanted to do business together again.

How that would work out, I didn't know. I was hoping he'd be man enough to understand about Czar and me.

I was doing sit-ups with my eyes closed, when I heard someone say my name. Without opening them, I knew it was Wesley.

"Why haven't you returned my calls?"

I stood up. "I'm sorry. I know I should have, but so much was going on. I was rarely home; at the hospital all the time. Then when my brother came out the coma, I really wasn't thinking about anyone other than him."

"So when did you get back?"

"Last night."

"Really? Damn! You could have called."

I didn't feel like being treated like a child, so I went off. "Well, you know what—I didn't; I could have, but I didn't."

"I'm going to let that go. I know I approached you wrong. I should have told you that I missed you, that I was concerned about you, that I'm glad your brother is okay."

"I'm still a little on edge."

"Well, that's understandable. Want to get together later?"

"Kavan has plans for us tonight."

He looked at me for a few seconds. "If I didn't know any better, I'd think you were avoiding me. How about I call you tomorrow and we have lunch or something?"

"You promise?"

"I promise."

"I'll be looking forward to it."

"Well, I'll let you get to your workout."

"Thanks."

When he was out of my vision, I grabbed my gym bag and went into the ladies' locker room to shower and change. As I was taking off my clothes, my cell phone started ringing. I was going to ignore it, but with all that had been happening, I thought it best to answer. I looked at the caller ID but didn't recognize the number. "Hello?"

"Hello, sexy," Czar said, bringing an immediate smile to my face.

"Hello, yourself." I wrapped my towel around me.

"Where are you?"

"In the gym."

"Do you want me to call you back?"

"I just saw Wesley."

"And?"

"He wants to go out."

"You told him no, didn't you?"

"I didn't know how. I told him no about tonight, but he would like to take me to lunch tomorrow."

"We need to tell him about us as soon as possible. No sense

leading him on. And I definitely don't want to be kept a secret. If we're going to see one another, I want it out in the
open."

"I don't want to be a secret any longer either."

"I'll be by tonight."

"Okay. I can't wait to see you."

"Ditto."

When we got off the phone, I didn't feel much better. I felt
like I should have told Wesley straight out that I couldn't see
him on any level other than business.

QUASSMIRAH

I was in the bathroom and heard every word. So that's why she wasn't calling Wesley back while she was in Jersey—she was seeing someone else.

Homeboy was pressed, acting all stressed, worrying about Ms. Layla, and she was getting her groove on. Well, you know what, I'm about to press up hard on a brother. I was trying to be respectful after the last incident with him and me, but not anymore.

I was attracted to Wesley. I mean, who wouldn't be?—brother is fine, built, smart and rich. What more could a girl ask for? He had all the qualities a sister looked for in a man. Also, I was tired of the dating scene and was ready to settle down. I was sure he wanted to settle down too; otherwise, he wouldn't be pressing up on Layla so hard.

LAYLA

I was walking out the locker room when I heard someone call my name. It sounded like Quassmirah. "Please, don't it let be her," I said to myself. Well, luck wasn't on my side.

"When did you get back?" she asked.

"Last night." I glanced at my watch, hoping she'd take a hint.

"How was the flight?"

"It was okay."

"How's your family?"

"Everyone is doing as well as can be expected. My brother is improving every day."

"That's good to hear. I'm happy for you."

"Thanks." I tried to walk away.

"Listen . . . wait for me to get my bag out the locker. I'll walk out with you."

There was no escaping her. I stood by the door as she grabbed her bag, and together we walked out.

"I overheard your conversation. Not that I was being nosy or anything. So who are you seeing?"

"I'd rather not say right now." Thank God, I didn't say Czar's name on the phone.

"Oh, so you're being secretive?"

"No, it's just that it's private right now, and I want to keep it that way."

"Have you told Wesley?"

"Why, Quassmirah?" I was tired of playing games. "I know you're interested in him. Don't let me hold you back from getting what could be yours." I wasn't stupid. That night we were at the club, she kept eyeing him with lust.

She was silent.

"Listen, a sister ain't mad at you. Wesley is cool as hell; he's just not my type. And as you know, I'm into someone else, so go for yours."

"Are you sure?"

"I'm absolutely positive." I glanced at my watch again. "I'm in a hurry; I'll catch you another time." I climbed in my car and drove home.

The truth
Needs to be told
Be bold
Speak your piece
Let it out
Say it gently with care
Don't shout
Cause a scene
Or demean
Love should be in the words

WHAT'S DONE IN THE DARK

When I arrived home, Kavan and TC were sitting on the couch having a cocktail. I plopped down next to them.

"Whew! It's been quite a day."

"Maybe you need a day at the spa," Kavan offered. "My treat."

I glanced over at my good friend and said, "I love you so much."

"I love you too."

"Should I leave the room?" TC joked.

We all laughed.

"Nah, Kavan is my boy; he's always there for me—I don't know what I would do without him."

"Damn, girl," Kavan said, "why you gotta get all sentimental on a brother? Didn't we do enough of that last night?"

The night before, Kavan and I sat up talking most of the night. I told him I felt like he was always there for me, always pulling for me, believing in me, and that what he offered me was nowhere near what I offered him.

"That's not true," he stated. "First of all, you were my first crush—actually, my first and only female crush. Secondly, you were the first person I told I was gay. And what did you do, you said, 'Oh,' and kept on going. You didn't make a big deal out of it; you didn't make me feel like an outcast; you just continued loving me. Then when I told you I was HIV-positive, you moved out here. I know you say you moved out here because you were ready for a change. That may be true, but I also know you moved out here to keep an eye on me."

I smiled when he said, "I thought that was my secret."

"So don't you dare say what I give you doesn't compare to what you give me—I could never ask for a better friend."

We fell asleep in his room hugged up, and I guess I let those emotions carry over to today.

"So, what's been up with your day?"

"I ran into Wesley. He wants to take me out tomorrow."

TC frowned.

"Right after I ran into him, Czar called me. We talked about telling Wesley about us together. I was in the locker room, thinking I was alone, but no—Quassmirah was in there and probably heard everything."

TC really frowned at the mention of her name and nudged Kavan.

"Okay, what's up, you two?"

TC started, "You want to know what's up?—I'll tell you what's up."

Kavan shot him a look that shut him up. "Remember when I told you I needed to talk to you about something? This was right before your brother's accident."

"Yeah."

"Well, TC overheard Wesley and Quassmirah on the phone that day you ran into him at Wesley's office, and according to him, they either have or had something going."

I looked over at TC. "Are you sure?"

"I'm positive. She said something like, 'You know you liked it,' and he said something like, 'I did, but it can't happen again.' It doesn't take a rocket scientist to figure out what they were speaking about."

"Are you okay?" Kavan asked.

"I'm more than okay." I stood up. I wasn't hurt or shocked; actually, I felt nothing.

"Are you sure?"

"Don't worry about me. I'm not surprised—I knew she was feeling him from the door. And it's not like we were best friends or anything; we only hung out a couple of times. Only thing is, I regret letting myself be open to him."

Kavan and TC stood up to hug me. "Well, we're here if you need us."

As I lay across my bed, I realized that I really wasn't upset. If anything, this was going to make it easier to break the news about me and Czar. I looked at the phone, picked it up, and called Czar to let him know what I had just learned.

Good riddance
Goodbye
Later
Peace
Maybe in another lifetime
Things could have been different
Although
I doubt it

A NEW BEGINNING

The next day couldn't arrive fast enough. I was ready to confront Wesley with this situation and move on with my life. So much had happened in the last six months. It felt like I was living someone else's life.

When I spoke to Czar and told him what I'd learned about Quassmirah and Wesley, he didn't seem too surprised. He said he suspected something, but since it was just a suspicion, he decided not to say anything for fear he might be wrong.

I was meeting Wesley across town at "Sharkies." The plan was for Czar to meet me there as well, and we'd break the news to Wesley about us *together*. I was nervous as hell not knowing how he would react.

"Take care of your business," Kavan told me as I walked out the door. "Call me if you need me."

I walked into the restaurant to find Wesley sitting at the table already.

When he spotted me, he stood up and pulled out my seat. "You look beautiful, as usual. Nice and cool."

"Thanks."

"So, would you like something to drink?"

I didn't answer him. I glanced towards the door, hoping Czar would hurry up and arrive. For one, I really didn't want to be there, I just wanted to hurry up and get this whole thing over with.

"Not yet."

"The video's coming out soon."

Now that piqued my interest. "Yeah, I'm excited about it."

He then pulled a disc out of his bag and handed it to me. "Here's an advance copy."

I smiled and thanked him.

"Are you glad to be back?"

"I don't know. On one hand I want to be in Jersey with my family, and on the other, I'm excited about my future on the West Coast."

I'd met with Mr. Irby, the producer, and he purchased the script. Now we had to wait and see what would come of it, if we could get a studio interested and make it into a film.

"I'm happy for you. It's good that—" He looked towards the door.

I followed his gaze and saw Czar coming walking towards us.

My face brightened up, and I tried like hell not to break out in a smile.

Wesley was smiling and putting out his hand to offer a shake. "What's up, man? This is a surprise."

Czar shook his hand and sat down. "Well, not really—I knew you would be here."

Wesley looked confused.

My heart was pounding. I cleared my throat. "Wesley, Czar and I were on the same plane when I was going to Jersey."

He raised his eyebrow. "Really?"

"We talked for some time and got to know one another."

"And?"

"We saw each other a couple of times on the East Coast."

I think he started to get the drift because a look of unease was on his face.

Czar said, "Look, man, I don't know how to tell you this

other than to come right out and say it . . . but we developed feelings for one another and we're going to continue seeing each other."

"So what the fuck is this? Are you asking me for my permission?"

"No. We just didn't want to go behind your back."

Wesley looked at Czar and back to me. Suddenly he broke out laughing. "This is unbelievable—my boy, my ace, my childhood friend, stabbing me in the back—I never thought you would pull some shit like this."

"What do you mean, stabbing you in the back? You're acting like you were being faithful to me, when all along you've been doing your thing."

"What the hell are you talking about? I've been sweating you from day one."

"Yeah, but you've been fuckin' Quassmirah—you think I don't know?"

"Man, please."

I wasn't letting him off the hook that easy. Plus, I needed to take the focus away from Czar and me. "So you're saying it's not true?"

"I don't have to justify it with an answer—think what you want to think." He stood up and faced Czar. "Do you really want to be me that bad?"

Czar didn't respond. We just watched him walk away— smack into Quassmirah, who was with a group of people.

This is getting better and better. I stood up. I wanted to confront her on being a fake-ass friend. But then Wesley said something to her.

She looked in our direction, said something to her companions, and walked out behind him.

"Good riddance." I looked over at Czar, who seemed to be in his own world. "Are you okay?" I asked him.

Czar

She asked me if I was okay, and I couldn't answer her. I wasn't sure how I was feeling. Wesley had been my boy for what seemed like forever, and I was letting a female come between us. This had never happened before, but Layla was special and worth it.

I should have backed off when I realized what I was feeling for her, but I couldn't, or I should say, I didn't want to. I'd never felt a connection like this before. The second I saw her, I wanted her to myself. And I knew it was more than physical, because we had yet to make love—that was probably why I couldn't pull myself away from her.

At the same time, I didn't want lose my friendship with Wesley. I was going to have a face-to-face talk with him. He was like a brother to me. *Maybe it's best to wait a few days.* I knew he was angry as hell right now and was the wrong person to deal with when angry.

"Don't worry about it," Layla said, interrupting my thoughts. "If your friendship means as much to him as it does to you, when he cools off, he'll deal with us being together."

See, that's what I'm talking about—homegirl knew what I was thinking without my even telling her.

Before moving on, I needed to settle things with Wesley.

Yes, he did something with Quassmirah and that was wrong, especially since he was trying to get with Layla. But that was no excuse. I couldn't dis a brother for that reason; I knew how I would feel if the shoe was on the other foot.

Layla and I ordered drinks and something to eat. We basically ate in silence, a comfortable silence, so it was all good.

A new relationship
About to start
Secrets
Hopes
Dreams
Learning likes and dislikes
Breaking up
Making up
Worth it
In the end
My lover
My friend

LAYLA—FINAL WORDS

That evening when I arrived home, Kavan asked me how it went.

"Quassmirah walked in when Wesley was leaving," I told him. "He said something to her, and the next thing you know, they're walking out the door together."

"Get out of here! How did he take the news about you and Czar?"

"Not too good. After he left, Czar was upset as well. He feels like he stabbed Wesley in the back."

"That's understandable."

"Maybe we shouldn't see each other until they work it out."

"That's mighty big of you."

I laughed. "I know, right? Waiting is nothing if it means good things will come, and Czar certainly qualifies as that."

Over the past year, I'd grown in all aspects of my life. It's said, God only gives you what you can handle and that every event in your life has a lesson. Well, after careful evaluation, here's what I'd learned: Tell people exactly what you expect from them, and be honest about it because no one's a mind reader. Never dishonor myself by living my life for those around me, but do what pleases me. That life was short, and since we don't know when our last day on earth is, we should make the most out of the days we have remaining. That it was a spectacular thing, not a selfish act, to live life on my own terms."

SIX MONTHS LATER

Czar and I were getting married, and Wesley was our best man. Another miracle, right?

Quassmirah?—well, her album was about to drop. We didn't associate on the friend level, but I did write the treatment for her first video. She called me one evening and apologized, told me her life story, and why she behaved the way she did.

I really wasn't mad at her. *Sometimes forgiveness is necessary for growth.*

Jaye was still married to his business and talking about "when I become a millionaire." I was glad I didn't wait for him, because the love that was in my life was so fulfilling.

My script was being made into a movie.

Keke and Ali were together, Justice settled down with one female, and my mother was dating.

Who knew what the next year was going to bring? All I knew was as long as I had the peace that surpassed all understanding, I was going to survive.

Love y'all! Peace.

Ms. Hunter is currently working on her third novel, *Turned Out,* and putting together a series of books for girls 9 to 12, and a fitness book for African American women.

Email the author at *selfofessence@aol.com*